Thirteen Cents

MODERN
African
Writing
from Ohio University Press

Ghirmai Negash, General Editor

This series brings the best African writing to an international audience. These groundbreaking novels, memoirs, and other literary works showcase the most talented writers of the African continent. The series also features works of significant historical and literary value translated into English for the first time. Moderately priced, the books chosen for the series are well crafted, original, and ideally suited for African studies classes, world literature classes, or any reader looking for compelling voices of diverse African perspectives.

Books in this series are published with support from the Ohio University National Resource Center for African Studies.

K. SELLO DUIKER

Thirteen Cents

Introduction by Shaun Viljoen

Ohio University Press

Athens

Other titles by this author:

The Quiet Violence of Dreams, Kwela Books, 2001
The Hidden Star, Umuzi, 2006

Ohio University Press, Athens, Ohio 45701
www.ohioswallow.com

Published in South Africa by Kwela Books,
an imprint of NB Publishers,
40 Heerengracht, Cape Town, South Africa
PO Box 6525, Roggebaai, 8012, South Africa
www.kwela.com

The moral right of the author has been asserted

First published by David Philip Publishers in 2000
First published by Kwela Books in 2013
First published by Ohio University Press in 2013

Library of Congress Cataloging-in-Publication Data
Duiker, K. Sello.
 Thirteen cents : a novel / K. Sello Duiker ; introduction by Shaun Viljoen.
  pages cm. — (Modern African Writing)
 Includes bibliographical references.
 ISBN 978-0-8214-2036-2 (pb : alk. paper) — ISBN 978-0-8214-4454-2
(electronic)
 1. Cape Town (South Africa)—Fiction. I. Title.
 PR9369.3.D74T54 2013
 823'.92—dc23

                        2013004758

K. Sello Duiker's *Thirteen Cents*

AN INTRODUCTION

Shaun Viljoen

ONE BREEZY NIGHT LATE IN NOVEMBER

One breezy night late in November
and after the April elections
Two friends stood outside
admiring the moon
'charming sky,' said the one
to the other
'What's even more charming is that
whitey has finally allowed himself
to be surrounded by darkey and they
seem to be getting on,' remarked
the other, staring into the night
At that moment a shooting star
blurred across the sky and both friends
saw it.
Wistful silence fell between them
the one not sure whether the other
had seen the meteorite. Then the
other opened: 'Perhaps it's not
about whitey and darkey anymore.'
The other assented.[1]

K. Sello Duiker's poem "One Breezy Night Late in November" imagines what the April 1994 democratic elections, the first in South Africa's history, meant for social relations that had been racialized since the landing of Dutch settlers in 1652 and hyperracialized since Afrikaner white minority rule took hold in 1948. In a reflective exchange between two friends in the poem, the initial thought of one about the historic turning point six months earlier asserts that the country will see racial reconciliation; the other responds unsurely, saying, "Perhaps it's not / about whitey and darkey anymore." In this tentative claim Duiker raises precisely what his astounding contribution to postapartheid literature has been—a provocative unsettling of the black and white, the categorical terms of engagement that marked human relations and writing under apartheid. Instead, as Meg Samuelson says of Duiker's first two novels, his work "interrogate[s] borders—whether social, national or ontological."[2]

The epiphanic moment in the poem occurs after "a shooting star / blurred across the sky" and a strange silence falls between the friends. As in the poem, all three of Duiker's novels—*Thirteen Cents*[3] (2000), *The Quiet Violence of Dreams* (2001), and *The Hidden Star* (published posthumously in 2006)—are marked by the presence of the supernatural, the surreal, the mythical, which layer and disrupt the real and comment on it. Narrative modes in the novels shift continuously between realist, hyperrealist, and surrealist, shunting the protagonist and the reader between different realms of consciousness and perception.

As in the poem, protagonists in the novels exist primarily as exceptional individuals, as an "I" rather than, as was the case with much (black) writing under apartheid in which the individual was metonymic of the greater (racial) community, as an "I" who is at the same time the "we." If anything, the voices in the poem represent themselves and are at a distance from both "whitey" and "darkey," identifying overtly with neither. There is an intimacy between the two friends, yet at the same time we feel a distance between the two, "the one not sure whether the other / had seen." All three novels present us with protagonists who are extraordinary individuals, with Azure in *Thirteen Cents* being the most clearly solitary and relentlessly individual character, who does not belong to any one place or to any social group, and who defies attempts to categorize him.

Thirteen Cents is a searing, disturbing coming-of-age account of Azure, a twelve-year-old orphan who has traveled from his home near Johannesburg to eke out an existence on the streets of post-1994 Cape Town. Azure lives in an underworld of shack dwellers, drug dealers, and gangsters and is exploited, often in most violent and demeaning ways, by all kinds of adults for their own ends. He survives through prostitution, selling sex to older men. In *The Quiet Violence of Dreams* Tshepo is a university student who at the start of the novel has been institutionalized for cannabis-induced psychosis and who, like the younger Azure, is an orphan and tries to find a sense of belonging in a hostile, dystopic postapartheid Cape Town. However, violence, exploitation, and bigoted attitudes that prevailed under apartheid continue to resurface in his quest to find a way of being in the world. Tshepo joins a brothel for male-to-male sex to earn money but also to explore his own homosexual impulses and need to create a fraternity or family. In the end, Tshepo leaves Cape Town for Johannesburg to try to find a better life. *The Hidden Star*, written for younger readers, is set in a township on the outskirts of Johannesburg and employs a child protagonist: the young girl Nolitye, who is invested with special powers by a magical stone, embarks on a quest to battle forces of greed and evil and restore her true family, displaced by these evil impostors. In the final novel the narrative shifts between the modes of African folktale and gritty realism, linking assertions of the ancestral to a strong sense of injustice in the contemporary social order. Duiker reiterates this link when he writes about the meaning of his own name. He dropped his first name, Kabelo, and adopted his second name, Sello, as the first name by which he wished to be known. Sello, his grandfather's name, is, he says, "a poetic name and it means lament! Someone who always cries out about things he sees—like injustice. It is a name that is very tied to ancestral voices."[4]

Thirteen Cents was published a mere six years after the first democratic elections, when Duiker was twenty-six years old, to critical acclaim and wide readership inside South Africa and abroad.[5] Of all the South African novels I have taught at undergraduate level, *Thirteen Cents* has proved to be the one that engages large numbers of young students. Is this because the novel speaks in such direct, frank, and contemporary terms about sex, sexuality, and addiction? Is it because of the manner in which we as readers are compelled to see the world from the point of view of the marginalized, abused, and exploited street boy narrator Azure, who represents what we see but dismiss every day of our waking life—those who are down and out and living on the far edges of monied, motorized, propertied society? Is it because, despite the horror and seemingly insurmountable odds stacked against him, Azure does not succumb to any of the dehumanizing forces that grind him down and the novel ends on a muted note of hope and the possibility of an alternative way of being in this world? This ability to engage a younger generation of readers seems to hold for places outside South Africa as well. According to Dutch writer Adriaan van Dis, who toured Indonesia in 2003 with Duiker as part of the Winternachten literary festival based in The Hague, Duiker's "frank and sincere stories about sex and the dark side of city life strongly spoke to the young Indonesians."[6]

Azure's position as a twelve-year-old who turns thirteen in the novel situates him on the threshold of the world of adults and subjects him to the rites of passage that induct him into particular forms of adulthood—in this case a particularly exploitative, destructive social order. He is a critical outsider to this world and continually resists incorporation—"Grownups are fucked up," he asserts (42). It is this significant turning from boyhood to manhood, this becoming thirteen to which the title alludes, that positions him as a critical commentator moving into and out of the dominant matrix of hierarchies and power. He is often drawn into and subject to this adult world and its values—"Men don't cry," he claims, "[a]nd since I'm nearly thirteen I mustn't cry. I must be strong. I must be a man" (26). This slippage into and out of the dominant social order across its ontological and spacial borderlines subjects the reader, as it does Azure, to experiences and perceptions of this order from both the intimacy of the inside and the estrangement of the outside. This contradictory fluidity is intensified by the first-person narrative Duiker deploys. Azure not only narrates his story himself but often does so in childlike egocentric vocabulary and syntax: the frequency of the narrating pronoun "I," probably the most frequent word in the text; the short, emotive sentences; and the clipped and spare dialogue. On the other hand, Azure's experiences are anything but childlike and innocent. The code-switching between languages and between colloquial and taboo registers attests to the child's harsh and very adult circumstances. The horrific verbal, emotional, and sexual abuse he is subject to stem from a world where self-interest, greed, addiction, and prejudice are rampant. Adults and their values have become the new oppressor, replacing the "whitey" who played that role in protest literature by black writers under apartheid. "[M]oney is everything" (18), Azure tells himself after he has been robbed of forty rands by the gangster pimp Allen, insightfully identifying the commodification and commercialization of social relations that rapidly overlaid race as the dominant line of fracture in postapartheid South Africa. As the title of the novel suggests, the destructive forces in Azure's worlds continually work to reduce him to near nothing, to a meager thirteen cents, to an object whose value is merely monetary.

Azure's physical appearance is as unsettling as is his narrative positioning. His blue eyes, to characters like the gang leader Gerald, are anomalous, given his dark skin, and provoke and interrogate stereotypical ideas of race, identity, and social hierarchy. Azure troubles the main racial categories of apartheid identity, "white," "coloured," and "black"—he is none of them and at the same time all of them.[7] Not only do his looks defy inherited racial classification, but his dress sense has no regard for conventions that are racially associated. Azure's childhood friend from Johannesburg and one of his few protectors, Vincent, warns him that Gerald is out to get him: "He thinks he's white because he's got straight hair and a light skin. If you show up with those shoes and your blue eyes, he'll kill you. He'll say, Who the fuck do you think you are? Trying to be white?" (39–40).

Gerald heads a hierarchy of destruction and evil equivalent to the evil witches MaMtonga and Ncitjana in *The Hidden Star*. His power resides in his control over others through relentless thuggery and brutality combined with his creation of financial, territorial, and emotional dependency that mimics supportive familial relations. After days of protracted physical torture and sexual violence inflicted on Azure by Gerald's minions like Sealy and Richard, Azure is expected to pay allegiance to Gerald, who takes on the role of father figure and protector, claiming in fact to have killed Azure's parents himself. The extraordinary power of the gangster is manifest in the manner in which he is able, in the mind of Azure and others, to transmute into the all-powerful dinosaur T-rex on the one hand, and into the form of ubiquitous pigeons on the other. To secure Azure as his own creation, Gerald insists he change his name to "Blue." But Gerald and his world cannot finally make Azure belong. Gerald's ignorance of the fact that "Blue" and "Azure" are essentially synonymous signifies his failure to rename the boy, and Gerald's final destruction marks Azure's triumph at resisting incorporation into Gerald's world and its debased values. In this regard, the final assertion of the novel, "My mother is dead. My father is dead," a disturbing refrain throughout the work that emphasizes Azure's orphaned and dislocated state, becomes a positive and hopeful statement against false belonging and inauthentic values that the impostor father represented. The unambiguously happy ending of *The Hidden Star* tells of Nolitye's final victory in casting off her false mother and being reunited with her real mother, whom she has rescued from the evil underworld: "'At last we're going home,' Nolitye says gratefully. 'Together'" (233).

Alongside the violence the young Azure experiences at the hands of adults, it is the sexualized nature of his existence on the streets that shocks and unsettles. Many readings of *Thirteen Cents* emphasize the fact that Azure engages in homosexual encounters with older men in order to earn money and survive on the streets. Azure confirms this reading when on numerous occasions he describes the encounters in graphic detail, but qualifies what is happening by stressing that he does what he does for the money, as a "trick." However, it is possible to nuance this reading with one that also sees the novel as a bildungsroman of the boy's sexuality in formation, with the exploration of inchoate sexuality, perhaps even homosexuality, as a subtext. The most protracted description of sex with a man is the one with the rich banker Mr Lebowitz. During this encounter, Azure distances himself and stresses that this is just another of many similar "tricks" he performs: "I know these bastards. I've done this a thousand times" (98). As he does on a number of occasions, he asserts a heteronormativity when he says he gets it up by thinking of Toni Braxton. Yet, on a number of occasions during this encounter, there are, despite the ominous suggestion of being filmed and watched, hints at pleasure-taking, both in the comfort and warmth of domestic space and even sexually. Azure's descriptions of moments of the encounter can be read as ambiguous and possibly, even subconsciously, taking pleasure. At one point also he feels a sense of pleasure during the encounter, but this is fleeting: "After a while the pleasure turns into sadness" (100). At another point, when they have a second go at it to the accompaniment of the "Winter" movement of Vivaldi's *Four Seasons*, Mr Lebowitz talks of trees without leaves, which takes Azure into a reverie of his own: "Trees, I know trees. I listen to the music. It is too much. . . . This guy is trying to open me up" (107). Azure here briefly reveals that there is something hidden within him that he is reluctant or unable to face but quickly reverts to a defense of this response as his way of protecting himself from exploitative adults like Mr Lebowitz and Joyce.

The closest we come to the young teenager reflecting more objectively on his sexuality and a possible alternative sexuality is when, toward the end of the novel, before his final ascent up the mountain, he interrogates his contradictory sexual impulses:

> I never dream of doing it with a woman. I'm not a moffie. One of the bastards once asked me if I was a moffie. And I told him that I'm not a moffie. But it's strange that I never dream of doing it with a woman, not even beautiful Toni Braxton. And the other guys are always saying that it happens to them. I just lie about it and say that it happens to me too even though it never has. (171–72)

The reiterated denials, "I'm not a moffie," suggest the young boy's repression of the disturbing possibility of its opposite—too traumatic a thought for someone his age and in his context to admit. By reading against the grain of the narrator's own claims, or finding contradictory moments on its surface, this bildungsroman then is as much about survival and a sense of self on the urban edges as it is about marginalized sexuality in formation (rather than an *assertion* of a particular set sexual identity). Like Azure, Duiker himself discourages reading the novel as being about "gay identity" when, in response to a question with regard to his own sexuality, he responded: "I'm a writer and interested in every aspect of human relations and identity. The whole thing is not an issue for me. My first novel, *Thirteen Cents*, did not have a gay character and neither will the third. I really don't want to be pigeon-holed."[8]

The explorations of homosexuality in Duiker's second novel, inflected with an array of other issues about young urban identity and belonging, makes such a subtextual reading of *Thirteen Cents* more plausible. He was in fact composing the two novels at the same time. Duiker's own interrogation in his fiction and poetry of the inherited boundaries of conventional identities and of limiting, categorical thinking, as well as his crisscrossing of languages and narrative modes in his work, would further corroborate such an interpretation. In addition, such a reading queers the dominant interpretation which insists that the homosexual encounters are, on Azure's side, simply to survive. It also challenges homophobic and moralistic readings of the novel, like that of Osita Ezeliora, whose emphasis on "survivalism" precludes any such exploration of sexuality in *Thirteen Cents* and condemns its exploration in the subsequent novel: "Duiker's transition from survivalism as the ideological propellant of homosexuality in *Thirteen Cents* to its glamorisation in *The Quiet Violence of Dreams* incites a perception of his narratives as literary sabotage of Africa's moral sanity, historical memory and cultural development."[9] The notion of homosexuality as "un-African" implicit in Ezeliora's view continues to undergird often violent repression of any sexual practice perceived as nonheteronormative in South Africa and on the African continent.[10]

Thirteen Cents is as much about Azure's interrogation and exploration of the temporal and spacial dimensions of his urban world as it is about the social and sexual dimensions. In the final third of the novel Azure makes two ascents up Table Mountain, which rises out of the heart of Cape Town and towers above it. These episodes are marked by insistent movement up and out of the cityscape and again down and into its innards as Azure tries to overcome the debilitating forces that engulf and consume him on the streets. Not only does his quest for a life of belonging beyond these destructive forces allow him to literally rise above them, but it also helps him imagine, through intensely sensory, hyperrealist[11] dream sequences, a different genealogy and a new city as the old is being destroyed before his very eyes.

On the mountain he experiences intense sensations and fantastical images, and his graphic and primordial dreams are shot through with elements of his real life. In an extended dream (the whole of chapter 17) he finds Saartjie, "a woman who looks like she lived a very long time ago" (139), whose name and figure invoke the ancestral Southern African Khoisan woman Saartjie (Sarah) Baartman.[12] She is at times maternal and protective of him, defending him against the omnipotent and diabolical T-rex, whom she claims is his father and her husband. She in turn is daughter to the terrifying Mantis who eats the sun, and she also claims Azure is the son of the sun. This private mythology and chain of being the boy dreams up is intermingled with his real past—T-rex is a figure from popular film culture and also a transmogrification of Gerald. In his vision Azure creates a new genealogy for himself to restore his dead mother and father. The imagined alternative is one deeply entangled with real history and African folklore, but also marked by contradiction, terror, and destruction, as is his real life. The destruction of the evil Gerald in the dream is paralleled by the destruction of the real

Gerald when Azure descends the mountain. The novel ends on an apocalyptic note; Azure, once again on top of the mountain, either imagines he sees or actually sees a giant explosion in the sky and fire falling to earth, and a tsunami sweeping away the city below. The ending, on the surface, is one of destruction and negation. But the mayhem also holds a moment of reassurance for both Azure and the reader: "I *know* what fear is . . . I have seen the centre of darkness . . . I *know* his secrets" (my emphases). The young boy has come through the apocalypse, and has attained greater self-knowledge and knowledge about his world. Azure's final assertion, "My mother is dead. My father is dead," is no longer merely an ever-present refrain; it is now also an acknowledged fact that the boy begins to grasp. Still completely alone, but with clarity of mind, he can, the ending suggests, begin again on the clean slate emerging beneath his feet.

* * *

Sello Duiker's life (1974–2005) straddled the dying days of apartheid and the post-1994 period. He was born in the iconic Johannesburg black township of Soweto, the place synonymous with the student revolts of 1976 that helped break apartheid's stranglehold on the country. His father and mother were part of the growing black middle class and both had degrees. His father's job with an international company relocated the family to England for a while.[13] Duiker credits his mother, an avid reader, with sparking his interest in books.[14] His parents of course wanted their firstborn to be well educated, sending him to a reputable Roman Catholic school in a neighboring "coloured" area. "It was at [this] time," he says, "[that] I was becoming aware of my race. I discovered that in the coloured community there was a lot of politics around hair, the smoothness and the colour."[15] As a schoolboy in his teens in the equally turbulent 1980s in Soweto he says he was "witnessing necklacing [and] kangaroo courts."[16] Duiker, like all South Africans, lived with the legacy of violence resulting from more than three and a half centuries of colonial and apartheid domination and divide-and-rule.

After school Duiker traveled for two years, first to the United States and then to Europe, working for a while as a dishwasher in Paris and also on a farm in France, and it was during this time that he started writing longer pieces of prose.[17] In Paris he visited many art exhibitions and, he says, was struck by the *Made in Heaven* exhibition of American artist Jeff Koons, in which explicit and graphic images blurred the borders between art and pornography.[18] When he returned home in 1995 he started a degree in journalism at Rhodes University in the Eastern Cape, which he felt would enable him to explore his desire to write. It was during his years as a student at Rhodes that he became interested in the lives of children living on the streets and started writing full-length fiction seriously. He tried but was unsuccessful at getting a manuscript published.[19]

He then moved to Cape Town in 1998, where he studied copywriting. During his two-year stay in the city he continued to explore his curiosity about street children, living, by chance Duiker says, with them for three and a half weeks when he was asked to help find a boy who went missing.[20] As a result of this long absence from his studies he was expelled from his college and in fact institutionalized in a psychiatric institution for two months. On his release he wrote the first draft of *Thirteen Cents* in less than two months.[21] The experience of living on the streets undoubtedly helped him capture street life in Cape Town with impressive verisimilitude—a hallmark of the novel which, like the work of Zimbabwean writer Dambudzo Marachera, shocks and provokes. At the same time he was working on the manuscript of *The Quiet Violence of Dreams*, which had already been accepted by Kwela Books but which his editor there, Annari van der Merwe, insisted he revise.[22] He returned to Johannesburg, where he completed *Thirteen Cents* and took up work as a freelance journalist and advertising copywriter, and also as a scriptwriter for the popular television soap operas *Backstage* and *Isidingo*.

While his life straddles the apartheid and postapartheid eras, Duiker's work has been firmly located by literary scholars as part of the postapartheid period,[23] dated often as starting in 1994 or even a bit earlier, in 1990, with the release of Nelson Mandela from prison. Much recent scholarship about South African letters has focused on attempts to characterize postapartheid society, literature, and culture and question what is distinctive in comparison to life, literature, and culture under apartheid. For Michael Chapman, this period of transition is marked by "anxieties and confusions about matters of identity in relation to massive socio-political change."[24]

Seminal to the literary debate have been the claims by writer and critic Njabulo S. Ndebele, whose essay "The Rediscovery of the Ordinary: Some New Writings in South Africa," first published in 1986, led the charge against black protest writing under apartheid, which he labeled "spectacular," with writers taking their cue from the "visible symbols of the overwhelmingly oppressive South African formation."[25] He characterized fiction by black South African writers as follows:

> The spectacular documents; it indicts implicitly; it is demonstrative, preferring exteriority to interiority; it keeps the larger issues of society in our minds, obliterating the details; it provokes identification through recognition and feeling rather than through observation and analytical thought; it calls for emotion rather than conviction; it establishes a vast sense of presence without offering intimate knowledge.[26]

Postapartheid literature moves away from the exterior binaries and the protesting voice to a preoccupation with the inner, the intimate, the individual, and the intermingled ordinary. It is, Andries Oliphant argues, a move away from "instrumentality" to "explore the new freedoms promised by the transition."[27] A new generation of novelists like Phaswane Mpe and Sello Duiker took up this newfound freedom and were seen as creative pioneers at the beginning of the new century, not only because of the focus of their fiction on contradictory entanglement of new and old, but also because they were seen to be "more formally innovative."[28]

In an attempt to characterize South African writing, both pre- and post-1994, David Attwell discusses the uneasy yet pervasive distinction often made between white writing and black writing, particularly under apartheid, and concludes that "tension, instability, and negotiation across a historical and cross-cultural divide permeate South African writing."[29] Duiker, speaking in interviews about his literary influences, points to a range of Southern African and international writers across lines of color and gives reasons for these identifications that have more often than not to do with questions of tension and instability. Bessie Head looms large in this regard, and Duiker says of her: "Bessie Head . . . [is] a 'coloured' South African writer. She was born from a white woman and rejected by her . . . by her own mother. Her strong identity as a 'coloured' woman is reflected in her writing."[30] He states that Head's novel *A Question of Power* inspired him to become a writer because "[h]ere is this person who was rejected by her community and took refuge wherever she could. I related to that, to her trying to find her feet."[31] Other literary works Duiker claims were important in shaping him as a youngster were Ben Okri's *The Famished Road*, Ayi Kwei Armah's *The Beautiful Ones Are Not Yet Born*, and the iconoclastic work of Dambudzo Marechera.[32] Duiker's Azure is remarkably similar to Okri's exceptional spirit child Azaro in *The Famished Road* (1991), and the Nigerian's negotiation of realist and surrealist styles clearly inspired the young South African. Sam Raditlhalo also suggests that Azure/Blue alludes to Toni Morrison's *The Bluest Eye* (1970).

Duiker epitomizes a new generation of South African writers who succeed more easily in creatively transgressing the old black/white divide that Attwell and others identify and attempt to bridge. The writers he names as making their mark range widely, asserting a cosmopolitanism and nonracialism rather than privileging merely the racial, nationalist, or Pan-Africanist. During Duiker's years of travel immediately after school he says he discovered the works of J. M. Coetzee, Breyten Breytenbach, and Doris Lessing. Duiker's work also invites wide-ranging comparison. There are striking similarities between Azure and Michael K, the protagonist of Coetzee's *The Life and Times of Michael K* (1983). A comparative study of the two novels would cut across the racial writing divide, as would, for example, a comparative study of a string of South African boy bildungsromans, from Es'kia Mphahlele's *Down Second Avenue* (1959) to Mark Behr's *The Smell of Apples* (1995), to *Thirteen Cents* and Michiel Heyns's *The Children's Day* (2002). A comparison between *Thirteen Cents* and Patricia Schonstein's *Skyline*, published in the same year as Duiker's novel, about a young girl's encounter with urban dwellers in Long Street, Cape Town, could invite a gendered analysis of postapartheid relations in the inner city. Such comparative, thematic analyses might go some way toward filling the gap identified by Rita Barnard: "There are, to date, surprisingly few critical works . . . that consider South African literature in a broad thematic way, and there are fewer still without the modifiers 'black' or 'white' inserted in the title."[33] Duiker's life, vision, and work certainly invite such nonracial explorations without diminishing the way questions of race still affect our lives.

Sello Duiker took his own life in January 2005, just about a month after his friend and fellow writer Phaswane Mpe had died.[34] A few days before Duiker's death, van der Merwe had sent him her edited version of *The Hidden Star* through the post, but it failed to reach him; his last novel ends by realizing the quest his first protagonist Azure had begun and fleetingly glimpsed from the top of the mountain: "home is never far away when you believe in it" (233).

A Note on K. Sello Duiker's Use of Language

Andries Oliphant outlines the effects of colonial and apartheid rule and ideology in South Africa on the domain of literature:

> Linguistically, Apartheid crystallised the colonial imperatives of segregation and white supremacy into rigid ethnic divisions between English and Afrikaans, on the one hand, as well as between these languages and the indigenous languages, on the other. This, as Msimang (1996:51) states, produced three distinct literary systems consisting of the two literatures in English and Afrikaans, separated from each other and placed at the apex and centre of the system, and the nine literatures in the African languages, located at the periphery and below English and Afrikaans.[35]

This separation and hierarchy of South African literature along language lines under apartheid begins to be challenged, to a certain extent, in the post-1994 period. Writers still choose one of the numerous languages used in South Africa as the language of their text (English, Afrikaans, isiZulu, and isiXhosa as the main ones), but there is now a greater mixing of languages, particularly in dialogue, in many creative works. Duiker continues to write in a tradition of Anglophone African writers, epitomized by Chinua Achebe, who choose to write in English rather than in an African language but at the same time make English serve their local and particular creative purpose. Nationally, Duiker follows in the South African novel tradition of writers like Peter Abrahams, Es'kia Mphahlele, Nadine Gordimer, Richard Rive, Alex La Guma, and J. M. Coetzee. Like these writers, Duiker inflects Standard South African English with other languages; in *Thirteen Cents* he combines English with regional dialect prevalent in the Cape that mixes English and Afrikaans with Sotho and Xhosa names and words in the narrative. Duiker can be seen as continuing the modern novel tradition in English, as Es'kia Mphahlele sees it, initiated by Peter Abrahams:

> Peter Abrahams . . . had become acquainted with the Negro authors of the Harlem Renaissance in the New York of the 1920s and the new consciousness that was to create a new kind of writing by Blacks. It was a rediscovery of an identity that echoed their African origins. Theirs was a style that captured the immediacy of an experience with vivid and concrete imagery, in all its harshness, in all its resonance of the fact of Black survival.[36]

Yet Duiker goes much further than any of these writers, crossing three conventional boundaries of fictional representation—he graphically depicts sex between child and adult, he does so specifically in relation to homosexual acts, and he uses expletives and the language of insult in a sustained manner that goes beyond merely inflecting the prose with local color.[37] Dehumanizing language is a violent assault on the human spirit, and Duiker attempts to capture this onslaught and resistance to it in authentic detail. He says: "I don't go out intentionally to shock. A lot of what I said could have been toned down. But violence is so much a part of our culture that if I had toned it down it wouldn't have been authentic."[38]

Unlike Mark Behr, for example, a South African novelist resident in the United States, who in his recent fiction *Kings of the Water* (2009) generates simultaneous translations of Afrikaans phrases within the text and a glossary of terms for his international readership, Duiker writes *Thirteen Cents* in the first instance for a younger, local audience, assuming his readers are familiar with the non-English terms. The absence of authorial mediation between the language of the story and readers also suggests Duiker's desire to construct an uncompromising, true-to-life account of a harsh reality. It gives his fiction a contemporary and naturalistic quality, much like the linguistic code-switching and cacophony of languages that one finds in popular South African TV soap operas and recent South African film.

The glossary that follows is intended to help readers decode the meaning and nuances of certain key terms in the novel not in English.

Glossary

babelas (isiZulu, slang)—hungover

ba batla borotho (Sesotho)—they want bread

baksheesh (Persian, slang)—tips and bribes

bergies (Afrikaans, slang)—literally mountain people; homeless people who take shelter on the slopes of Table Mountain or on Cape Town city streets

braai (Afrikaans)—cookout, barbecue

buttons (informal)—Mandrax, Quaaludes

cherrie (Afrikaans, slang)—young woman or girlfriend

daai glad hare (Afrikaans)—that smooth hair

dankie (Afrikaans)—thank you

deurmekaar (Afrikaans)—crazy

eish (slang)—oh dear

gemors (Afrikaans)—a mess, confusion

hey voetsek (Afrikaans)—fuck off

julle fokken (Afrikaans)—your fucking

kaffir (derogatory)—native, black man/woman

kak (Afrikaans)—shit

kwaito (derived from Afrikaans)—South African mix of township hip hop, reggae, house music *laaitie* (Afrikaans, slang)—young boy

los hom (Afrikaans)—let him go, leave him alone

maar (Afrikaans)—but

mageu (isiZulu)—traditional drink made from fermented maize

mahala (South African slang)—for free, free of charge

makwerekwere (isiXhosa, derogatory)—foreigners, outsiders,
   non-South Africans

mannetjies (Afrikaans)—little men

meisietjie (Afrikaans)—girl

mense (Afrikaans)—people

mnqusho (isiXhosa)—traditional meal of hominy-like samp
   (dried corn kernels that are soaked and coarsely pounded;
   generally cooked with beans)

moegoe (Afrikaans slang)—dope, fool, idiot

moer (Afrikaans, threatening)—to beat up; to fuck up

moffie (Afrikaans, derogatory)—faggot

naai (Afrikaans, slang)—one of many words for having sex;
   screw, poke

ouens (Afrikaans)—guys

oupa (Afrikaans)—grandfather

outie (Afrikaans, slang)—wiseguy

Pagad mense—*PAGAD*—People against Gangsterism and Drugs, Islamic vigilante group in Cape Town

phuza-face (isiZulu, slang)—an alcoholic

piel (Afrikaans, slang)—dick, penis

poes (Afrikaans, derogatory)—cunt

skyf (Afrikaans)—cigarette, puff, joint

spaza (slang)—small convenience store in township or rural area

stop / zol / pilletjie (Afrikaans slang)—a joint

suig (Afrikaans)—suck

thula (isiZulu)—quiet or hush

Vaalie mense (Afrikaans slang)—(white) people from the old Transvaal province

veldskoene—(Afrikaans) usually handmade soft shoes made from untanned leather, field shoes

wena—(isiXhosa) you

windgat—(Afrikaans) windbag, someone who talks and boasts too much

yessus—from Jesus, meaning damn

voetsek—fuck

Notes

1. K. Sello Duiker, "One Breezy Night Late in November," first published in *Words Gone Two Soon: A Tribute to Phaswane Mpe and K. Sello Duiker*, edited by Mbulelo Vizikhungo Mzamane (Pretoria: Umgangatho, 2005), 62, and reprinted with the kind permission of the Duiker family.

2. Samuelson, "Crossing Borders with Words," 199.

3. A number of scholars, and Duiker himself, use lowercase letters when citing the title of this novel, the form given on the cover of the David Philip publication. Others, myself included, have chosen to standardize the title using conventional capitalization.

4. In a letter to Mories Römkens, quoted in Annari van der Merwe's "Tribute" in Mzamane, *Words Gone Two Soon*, 12–13.

5. For *Thirteen Cents* Duiker won the 2001 Commonwealth Writers Prize for Best First Book in the Africa Region. For *The Quiet Violence of Dreams* he was awarded the 2001 Herman Charles Bosman Prize.

6. Quoted in van der Merwe, "Tribute," 12.

7. For more on Duiker's nonracialism, see Shaun Viljoen's "Non-Racialism Remains a Fiction."

8. "Interview with Victor Lackay," in Mzamane, *Words Gone Two Soon*, 20.

9. Ezeliora, "The Novels of K. Sello Duiker and Phaswane Mpe," in Mzamane, *Words Gone Two Soon*, 173.

10. For arguments that counter the homogenizing and essentialist view that certain sexualities are "un-African" see various chapters in *African Sexualities: A Reader*, edited by Sylvia Tamale.

11. I use the term "hyperrealist" to describe a narrative style that deploys graphic, extraordinary, and gritty language, situations, and imagery in sustained ways to represent and comment on a particular reality.

12. Saartjie Baartman was taken from Cape Town to Europe in 1807 and exhibited in Britain and France as the "Hottentot

Venus," a sexual and racial exotic because of the size and shape of her buttocks. Her remains were returned to South Africa in 2006. Many scholars see Baartman's story as exemplifying colonial fascination with the African woman as the sexualized exotic.

13. Duiker, "'The Last Word': Sello Duiker," in Mzamane, *Words Gone Two Soon*, 27.

14. Ibid., 28.

15. "Interview with Bafana Khumalo," in Mzamane, *Words Gone Two Soon*, 22.

16. "Interview with Victor Lackay," 19.

17. Duiker, "'The Last Word': Sello Duiker," 27.

18. Interview by Mikkel Simonsen, in Simonsen, "Realising the Gift," 6.

19. "Interview with Bafana Khumalo," 23.

20. "Interview with Victor Lackay," 20.

21. Duiker, "'The Last Word': Sello Duiker," 28.

22. Van der Merwe, "Tribute," 6. Van der Merwe played a seminal role in Duiker's life as a writer, becoming a friend and a champion of Duiker's work and taking on responsibility for editing his last novel for publication after his death.

23. The term "postapartheid" is widely used to talk about South African literature after 1990, or 1994. Reservations about the appropriateness of the term stem from the fact that while racial discrimination ceased to have any legal basis post-1994 and especially post-1996 (when the new "nonracial" South African constitution was installed), many of the social features of life under apartheid—the encampment of black people in locations in periurban areas, the widespread poverty and unemployment among black people, a dysfunctional school system in black areas—persist to the present. In addition, as Rita Barnard claims about the geographies of South African cities after apartheid, "old divisions are now articulated and justified in new terms" (*Apartheid and Beyond*, 67). An example of this is the manner in which the rapid gentrification of the inner Cape Town has made it accessible for the wealthier, mainly white populace and forced

out and kept out the poorer, mainly nonwhite citizens who were removed from their city homes by apartheid legislation.

24. Chapman, *Southern African Literatures*, xiv.

25. Ndebele, "The Rediscovery of the Ordinary," 31.

26. Ibid., 41.

27. Oliphant, "A Changing Topography," 236.

28. Cornwell, Klopper, and MacKenzie, *The Columbia Guide to South African Literature in English since 1945*, 32.

29. Attwell, *Rewriting Modernity*, 16.

30. "Interview with Victor Lackay," 21.

31. "Interview with Bafana Khumalo," 23.

32. Duiker, "'The Last Word': Sello Duiker," 27; interview by Simonsen, 8.

33. Barnard, *Apartheid and Beyond*, 4.

34. In a tribute to Duiker, Sam Raditlhalo gives more speculative detail about the death: "Duiker, who suffered from bipolar affective disorder, committed suicide in a state of depression he attributed to his mood-stabilising medication, which he felt was 'taking too great a toll on his artistic creativity and joie de vivre' (van der Merwe, 2005). He may have died by his own hand, but there is no doubt that what killed him was a potentially lethal illness that is stigmatised, little understood and often poorly managed." Raditlhalo, "'The Travelling Salesman,'" 96.

35. Oliphant, "A Changing Topography," 231.

36. Mphalele, *Es'kia Continued*, 36.

37. A comparison with the language of the gangster in short stories by Richard Rive, such as "Dagga-smoker's Dream" or "Rain," written in the 1950s, will reveal the extent to which Duiker goes to capture authenticity rather than local color.

38. Interview by Simonsen, 11.

Works Cited

Attwell, David. *Rewriting Modernity: Studies in Black South African Literary History.* Athens: Ohio University Press, 2006.

Barnard, Rita. *Apartheid and Beyond: South African Writers and the Politics of Place.* Oxford: Oxford University Press, 2007.

Chapman, Michael. *Southern African Literatures.* Scottsville: University of Natal Press, 2003. First published 1996 by Longman.

Cornwell, Gareth, Dirk Klopper, and Craig MacKenzie. *The Columbia Guide to South African Literature in English Since 1945.* New York: Columbia University Press, 2009.

Duiker, K. Sello. *The Hidden Star.* Cape Town: Kwela, 2006.

———. "Interview with Bafana Khumalo." In Mzamane, *Words Gone Two Soon,* 22–23.

———. "Interview with Victor Lackay (courtesy of co-author Carl Collison): 'I'm a Travelling Salesman.'" In Mzamane, *Words Gone Two Soon,* 19–21.

———. "'The Last Word': Sello Duiker." In Mzamane, *Words Gone Two Soon,* 27–30.

———. "One Breezy Night Late in November." In Mzamane, *Words Gone Two Soon,* 62.

———. *The Quiet Violence of Dreams.* Cape Town: Kwela, 2001.

———. *Thirteen Cents.* Cape Town: David Philip, 2000.

Ezeliora, Osita. "The Novels of K. Sello Duiker and Phaswane Mpe." In Mzamane, *Words Gone Two Soon,* 164–75.

Mphahlele, Es'kia. *Es'kia Continued: Literary Appreciation, Education, African Humanism and Culture, Social Consciousness.* Johannesburg: Stainbank, 2004.

Mzamane, Mbulelo Vizikhungo, ed. *Words Gone Two Soon: A Tribute to Phaswane Mpe and K. Sello Duiker.* Pretoria: Umgangatho, 2005.

Ndebele, Njabulo S. "The Rediscovery of the Ordinary: Some New Writings in South Africa." *Journal of Southern African Studies* 12, no. 2 (1986): 143–57. Reprinted in Njabulo S. Ndebele, *Rediscovery of the Ordinary: Essays on South African Literature and Culture,* 31–54. Scottsville: University of KwaZulu-Natal Press, 2006.

Oliphant, Andries Walter. "A Changing Topography: Tracing Some Recent Developments in South African Writing." In Mzamane, *Words Gone Two Soon,* 230–50.

Raditlhalo, Sam. "'The Travelling Salesman': A Tribute to K. Sello Duiker: 1974–2005." *Feminist Africa* 5 (2005): 96–104.

Rive, Richard. "Dagga-smoker's Dream." In *Advance, Retreat: Selected Short Stories*, 5–9. Cape Town: David Philip, 1989. First published 1983.

———. "Rain." In *Advance, Retreat: Selected Short Stories*, 11–19. Cape Town: David Philip, 1989. First published 1983.

Samuelson, Meg. "Crossing Borders with Words: Sello Duiker, Phaswane Mpe and Yvonne Vera." In Mzamane, *Words Gone Two Soon*, 196–201.

Simonsen, Mikkel. "Realising the Gift: K. S. Duiker's Shades of Identity." Unpublished Honours paper, University of Stellenbosch, 2004.

Tamale, Sylvia, ed. *African Sexualities: A Reader.* Nairobi: Pambazuka, 2011.

van der Merwe, Annari. "Tribute." In Mzamane, *Words Gone Two Soon*, 5–14.

van Dis, Adriaan. "Tributes." In Mzamane, *Words Gone Two Soon*, 11–12.

Viljoen, Shaun. "Non-Racialism Remains a Fiction: Richard Rive's *'Buckingham Palace,' District Six* and K. Sello Duiker's *The Quiet Violence of Dreams.*" *English Academy Review* 18, no. 1 (2001): 46–53.

1

My name is Azure. *Ah-zoo-ray.* That's how you say it. My mother gave me that name. It's the only thing I have left from her.

I have blue eyes and a dark skin. I'm used to people staring at me, mostly grown-ups. When I was at school children used to beat me up because I had blue eyes. They hated me for it. But now children just take one look at me and then they either say something nasty or smile. But grown-ups, they pierce you with their stare.

I live alone. The streets of Sea Point are my home. But I'm almost a man, I'm nearly thirteen years old. That means I know where to find food that hasn't seen too many ants and flies in Camps Bay or Clifton. That is if there aren't any policemen patrolling the streets. They don't like us much. Or if I fancy some fruit then I go to the station where the coloured fruit-sellers work. I don't like them much because they are always yelling at us to move away. Most of them throw away fruit instead of giving it to us. But I'm not stupid. I know that they put funny things in the dustbins where we go scratching for food. I can smell their evil. I know a few kids who are under their evil spell. They make them walk the night spreading their evil. And some of them are so deep into their evil they can change shape. They can become rats or pigeons. Pigeons are also rats, they just have wings. And once you become a rat they make you do ugly things in sewers and in the dark. It's true. It happens. I've seen it.

But like I said I'm almost a man. I can take care of myself. "Julle fokken mannetjies moet skool toe gaan," the fruit-sellers yell. It's easy for them to say that. I lost my parents three years ago. Papa was bad with money and got Mama in trouble. The day they killed him I was away at school. I came back to our shack only to find them in a pool of blood. That was three years ago. That was the last time I went to school.

I walk a lot. My feet are tough and rough underneath. But I'm clean. Every morning I take a bath at the beach. I wash with sea water. Sometimes I use a sponge or if I can't find one I use an old rag. It's just as good. Then I rinse off the sea water at the tap. It's not that bad washing with cold water. It's like anything – you get used to it.

My friend Bafana can't believe that I saw my dead parents and didn't freak out. But I told him. I cried and then it was over. No one was going to take care of me. He's still a laaitie, Bafana, only nine years old and he's on the streets. And he is naughty. He has a home to go back to in Langa but he chooses to roam the streets. He likes sniffing glue and smoking buttons when he has money. I don't like that stuff, it makes my head sore. But I like smoking ganja, quite a lot actually. Now Bafana when he smokes glue and buttons he becomes an animal, really. He starts grunting and doesn't speak much and he messes his pants. So whenever I see him smoking that stuff I beat him. I once beat him so badly he had to go to Groote Schuur to get stitched. I don't like that stuff. It just does terrible things to your body.

I sleep in Sea Point near the swimming pool because it's the safest place to be at night. In town there are too many pimps and gangsters. I don't want to make my money like them. So during the day I help park cars in Cape Town. It's not easy work. You have to get there early. Sometimes you have to fight for your spot. The older ones leave us alone, they get all the choice parking spots in the centre of town. It's like that. I don't ask questions.

I help people park cars and wash them if the owners let me. If you wash their car before you ask them most times they just swear at you because you're a laaitie and they are big. You see it's like that. That's how it works here. You must always act like a grown-up. You must speak like them. That means when you speak to a grown-up in town you must look at them in the eyes and use a loud voice because if you speak softly they will swear at you. You must also be clean because grown-ups are always clean. And you must never talk to them like you talk to a laaitie. Like I can't talk to them the way I talk to Bafana. I must always say "Sir" or "Madam". It's like saying "Magents" except it's for grown-ups. And when I can remember I say "please" and "thank you". Those two words are like magic, my secret. They've made me nice money every time I used them with a smile.

I work near a takeaway shop called Subway. On a good day I can make enough money to buy half a loaf of white bread with chips and Coke and still have two rands left over to buy a stop from Liesel who stays under the bridge.

She's the only grown-up I trust because she asks me for money and always pays me back a week later. I also like her because she let me see how a woman looks like naked. She doesn't tell lies, Liesel, not like the other people who stay under the bridge. All the skollies, gangsters and drunks with phuza-face also stay there.

Poor Liesel. I know what she does to make money. It's not easy. That's why I never ask her about it. And when she has a bruise or a cut under her lip I don't say anything. I just pretend that things are like always, the same. We talk about kwaito and whether the Rasta who brings her stop will get good stuff like Malawi gold or Mpondo and we talk about other things. I like her a lot but she's not my cherrie. She's got her own outie. I don't like him much. He's a member of the Hard Livings gang.

2

Morning creeps in slowly. Bafana sleeps curled in a half-moon beside me. I get up to take a pee. I rub my eyes and let out a yawn as I piss. We sleep at the far corner of the beach. Above us is the swimming pool. It is too early for the public toilets to be open so I go a little further up the beach and do my business near a drain. Deep orange clouds cover the sky. Seagulls fly by and cry.

"Bafana, son, get up, we need to get breakfast." I poke him. "Bafana . . . Bafana."

I go on like this for about five minutes before he gets up.

"Wena, you must stop taking those stupid drugs. They are fucking you up. Look at you, you can't even get up. You're lucky it's me. Somebody will think you're dead."

He moans and looks at me with a skew face.

"I'm hungry," he mumbles.

"Ja, shuddup, you know what you have to do."

"Wena, and your stupid rules."

I slap the back of his head and he clicks his tongue at me.

"The sun is already out, hurry up. I'm also hungry."

We take off our clothes and go towards the water only dressed in our shorts.

"Don't make me drag you in there, son, we go through this every morning."

"Yessus! Who said I have to wash every day?"

"Hey voetsek! Don't give me shit. You know my rules. If you want to stay with me you have to wash. Now fuck off," I say and push him into the water.

He shrieks.

"Thula, man. People are still sleeping. This isn't town."

I only go in up to my ankles and watch him scrubbing with a cloth.

"Do it properly," I warn him.

"Eish maar, wena."

After a while I let him go out and rinse off at the tap. He sits on a rock and dries off in the sun while I bathe. I think about all the things I plan to do today while I wash. My eyes sting from the salt water.

After washing we get dressed and go up Main Road. I know a woman who works at a restaurant called La Perla. She usually leaves leftovers for us near a bush. I'm the only one who gets the food because I don't trust Bafana. He's still a laaitie and sometimes he gets desperate when he's on his stupid drugs. I've worked too hard to see someone mess up a regular meal for me. She's nice, the auntie who gets the food for me. Her name is Joyce but she likes me to call her Auntie. She says I remind her of her son in Lichtenburg. Anyway, in exchange for the meal she sends me to the shop to do her small groceries. Or sometimes she sends me to the Post Office or she gives me money to buy her *Die Burger*. There's nothing for mahala with grown-ups. You always have to do something in return. But I don't mind because Joyce is nice.

We sit on a balcony overlooking the pool and eat. Joyce always packs the food into those McDonald's plastic things and gives us spoons. We watch the morning swimmers do their lengths. As always the pool is a clear blue-sky colour. I love to swim and I'm dying to swim in that pool. But six bucks is a lot of money and you have to have a towel.

"We need to make some baksheesh today," Bafana finally says after he's had enough to eat.

"Ja, ja. What do you plan on doing?"

"But I thought we're a team."

"Voetsek! Don't talk rubbish. You do this every day. When are you going to get it into your head that I'm not your mother? I'm only doing you a favour by letting you sleep by me. You know what would happen to you otherwise. You and your stupid drugs. Now you want me to work with you so you can buy your stupid drugs. You're full of kak. Fuck off!" I push him and walk off towards the park and leave him to fend for himself.

I'm not his father, I say to myself. That laaitie is getting under my armpit, under my soft spot. I mustn't let that happen, I tell myself. I've seen too many kids die and disappear. There's

7

no point in getting too close. Just now he gets an overdose from his stupid drugs. And then what? Now I must walk around crying because this stupid boy who has a home ran away to kill himself with drugs. I'm not stupid, man. If he wants to do grown-up things then I must leave him. He wants to play with fire, let him.

I walk towards a fountain near some toilets. Grown-ups are strange people. How can they put a fountain for drinking water outside a toilet? And I mean right outside the Men's toilet. I drink some water and fill a plastic container, one of those fancy ones that sell fancy water. I wonder if that water tastes any different.

I walk further along the beach till I come to the moffie part of the beach. I sit on a bench and wait for a trick. I sit a long while before I hear someone whistling. Soon I'm walking back with a white man to his flat. When we get inside the lift he tells me to take off my shoes. I know the routine. Once inside his flat he will expect me to strip off at the door. We go in and I begin to take off my clothes at the kitchen door.

"What's your name?" he asks as he stares at my nakedness.
"Azure."

"Interesting name," he says drawn by my blue eyes.

I grin while he strokes my face. He leads me through the house and we make our way to the bathroom. The house is clean and warm. I walk carefully as though careless footsteps might disrupt the cleanliness. He takes off his clothes and his piel bounces in front. I shudder to look at it and wait for him to lead me into the shower. But I know his type, he probably just wants to play, nothing else.

"Why are you so quiet?" he says while the water runs.

"I'm just listening."

"To what?"

"Your house. It's so quiet."

"Oh that. Do you want me to put on some music?"

"No, I like it like this. Please."

He rubs the soap quickly between his hands and slides his hands on my back and bum. I'm forced to smile. That's what they expect. Grown-ups, I know their games. I smile. He slides his hands around my waist and touches my belly. Not so quickly, I say to myself before he goes any lower. I bend down to pick up the soap.

He gets out to dry himself and leaves me with a few minutes of heaven with warm water and fresh-smelling soap. I slide the soap all over my body, blowing bubbles when I can, a silly grin that only I can enjoy on my face. The water falls on me with pleasure. I tingle with cleanliness.

"Are you coming? I'm waiting," he says after a while.

They don't like you to know their names, in case you bump into them in the street. Most times they don't even nod or say hi, they walk past as if they don't know you.

"Come now, I've got things to do," he says in a serious grown-up voice.

I turn off the taps and shake off the water still clinging to me. He slides the door open and hands me a towel. A fresh-smelling light blue towel. I sigh with pleasure as I dry myself. His eyes follow my every move.

"Come now, we must get on with it," he says a little anxiously and grabs the towel. I walk behind him as we both walk naked towards the bedroom. Morning light pours in through fancy curtains with slits. Above his bed there is a framed poster of a young boy taking a piss. There's a dreamy look in his eyes as he looks towards us while pissing. I look around the neat room with awe while his piel begins to grow.

"Lie down," he says and lays me beside him. Then he starts playing with me. I have to concentrate hard to get excited. I think of Toni Braxton and Mary J Blige. They usually do the trick for me.

We use a lot of baby oil. I close my eyes while he moans a lot.

"Tell me when you're going to come," he says politely, strangely.

"I can come any time. I was waiting for you."

"In that case let's come."

He stands over me while I lie down and we both masturbate. After a while his eyes roll into their whites and I feel warm drops across my chest and face. He hands me a towel to dry myself.

With a wallet in his hand we go to the kitchen.

"You did good," he says and hands me a twenty-rand note. Peanuts. I've earned fifty bucks from a single trick. But I know not to get greedy. He could become a regular. I get dressed quickly and let myself out. Just before going out the door to the flats another white man looks at me with come-to-bed eyes. A lot younger than the other guy. I decide to follow him. He stays on the first floor.

"Don't worry about that," he says as I start to undo my shirt. "You don't have to take off your clothes. I just want to be sucked off. Don't worry, I won't come in your mouth."

It doesn't take long before I make him come on his bare chest. He pays me forty bucks and sees me out of the flat.

3

I need a new pair of shoes, I say to myself as I count the money. Joyce is not working, she only works nights. I decide to go to her small flat which she shares with another auntie. At the door she is only too happy to see me.

"Dankie vir die kos, Antie, ek was baie honger. Where's Auntie Bertha?"

"She went home for a few days. You know how she gets homesick. Cape Town can be so lonely," she says, walking around in her lazy flip-flops.

"Anyway, I've got some money and I thought maybe you could put it into my bank."

Joyce understands banks and how they work. Me, I have forgotten even how to hold a pen, so how can I go to the bank myself? Grown-ups ask many questions there. You must remember when you were born and exactly how old you are. You must have an address and it must be one that doesn't keep changing. Like you must stay in the same spot for say maybe five years and when you move you must tell the bank. They must know everything about your movements. Like how many homes you have and whom must they call when you want to do something with your money. If you ask me they are a bit like gangsters, they want to know everything so that you cannot run away from them. And you must have an ID and a job that pays you regularly. And every time you put in money they make money for you by lending out your money. They are very clever people who work at banks. That's what Joyce says. She says she ordered a banking place for me at First National Bank and that all my money is going to be safe there. Every time I make money I give her some and she puts it away for me in the safe. It's my plan to do something with it one day. I'm not sure what I can do with it or how much I have saved but I have a feeling that it will come in handy one day.

Today I give her twenty bucks and keep the rest. What I like about Joyce is that she never asks me how I make my money. In fact, unlike most grown-ups she doesn't ask too many questions. She's only too happy to be sitting at the window sewing or doing something with her hands. Sometimes I just sit there with her and we say nothing to each other for hours. It's so peaceful.

Sometimes, when she's not feeling like an auntie, she lets me smoke a cigarette with her but that doesn't happen often. She never beats me but jeez she can get very angry with me, especially when my clothes are dirty. When I have enough money, because food always comes first, I buy soap and wash my clothes at a public toilet. I wash them one at a time. T-shirt first and when it has dried I wash my socks and when they've dried I wash my pants but I wear them wet till they dry in the sun from all the walking I do.

Joyce pours me a cup of tea. I sit on the floor beside her and we listen to her wireless. On the news Pagad is on the loose again. Another policeman was shot dead in his home.

"You know, Zu-zu, these Pagad mense they say they are God's people but they preach the devil's work."

"Yes, Auntie."

"You must stay away from them, you hear, Zu-zu."

"Yes, Auntie."

"And the gangsters. If I ever hear that you are a member of a gang you can forget about Auntie ever giving you food or banking your money. Do you hear me?"

"Me, Auntie, I'm not like them. I'm not a moegoe."

"You must promise me this, Zu-zu. Say you'll never be a member," she says and looks at me with a schoolteacher's serious eyes.

"I promise, Auntie."

"No, you mustn't promise. Say it. I want to hear you say it."

"I promise not to be a member, Auntie."

"That's good, Zu-zu, that's good."

We sit in silence for a while and listen to the rest of the news. After a while I tell Auntie that I must be on my way.

I go to Green Point where Allen works as a pimp. I find him standing under a large blue-gum tree talking to one of his white girls. They are arguing about something. I stand back because I know Allen's temper. He's killed someone before and I saw the whole thing happen. Knowing him has actually helped me a lot on the streets. I can't say that we are friends. But if I'm ever in trouble I just have to say that I know Allen and I'm usually left alone.

"Why must I fucking work today?" she yells at him, her pupils like saucers. Stupid woman, she's high.

"Because I told you so, bitch. Who the fuck do you think you are? Don't pull this shit on me just because you've just had your rock."

"I don't see why I have to work today. I haven't had a day off in two weeks, Allen. What about my pussy?"

"Fuck you," he punches her and she falls flat on her face in the street. A car drives near her and hoots at Allen. "You and your pussy, fuck you. You're full of shit." He goes on and grabs her by the hair.

That's the problem with the white bitches. I find that they never know when to shut up and here the ouens don't give them a chance. They are heavy-handed. They just whack. And if that doesn't do it, they naai and then they fuck them up even more.

"You weren't complaining yesterday when that client paid you a three hundred rand tip. Don't think I don't know about that, bitch. I know about it. You can't hide anything from me, meisietjie. Daai glad hare, it does nothing for me. This isn't

Joburg," he continues slapping her. "I'm going to moer you for your mouth, you must learn when to shut up."

By this time she has a serious cut under her left eye and bruises all over her face. Her clothes are also torn. He grabs her by the scruff and bundles her to his flat which is on the same road. People walk by.

"What the fuck do you want?" he says as he walks past me.

I show him forty bucks. That's the only thing Allen understands best – money. He doesn't answer. He just calls me with his head. The white girl is bleeding but she doesn't cry.

"I should naai you for all the shit you cause, you stupid bitch," he says and throws her on the couch that looks flea-ridden. The cats scurry away. She doesn't say anything.

"Go clean up before I fuck you up again," he yells, the devil in his eyes. He kicks her hard in the ass as she gets up. She falls on her face and starts crying.

"Get up, you cunt! Poes! Fokken naai!"

She gets up slowly and goes to the bathroom.

"Now what the fuck do you want? And who said you could sit down? Fuck off your naai, get up," he turns to me.

"Allen, I need shoes," I say looking at his feet.

"Fuck off, why didn't you come yesterday?"

I wait for him to slap me but he doesn't.

"Hey, what's your fucking problem? Look at me when I'm talking to you." He straightens my head by the chin.

I look at him, hiding the terror in my eyes.

Unexpectedly, he smiles and shows off his mouth of mostly gold fillings.

"You're my my laaitie, you know that? Where's your money?"

I give him the moistened notes.

"Wait here," he says. "Don't sit. I'll have a look in the bedroom."

On the floor around me there are boxes of stolen items, things that Allen or whoever it was got from house breaking. A pair of Reebok tackies that look like my size stare at me from the corner. Allen returns with ten-rand flip-flops. He throws them at me and says I must return in three days' time to get proper shoes. What he means is that I must return in three days' time with more money. And when I do I must not say anything about today, otherwise he will beat the living shit out of me. He's like that, Allen; you must never remind him of anything. He knows everything. I take off my shoes with holes at the bottom and put on the thin strops. Give me those ones, he orders me. I nearly hesitate but give him. What is he going to do with them? I walk out his flat and try not to think of my money as wasted but as protection money.

I can walk a little safer knowing that Allen has my money. Money is his language. It's the only thing he remembers, everything else is unimportant. I wouldn't be surprised tomorrow if he asked that girl who beat her up. Of course she would be forced to say that someone else beat her up in fear of upsetting him again. And then another stupid argument would start and more blood and tears. He's totally messed up, Allen. I don't know if he's crazy or just likes playing games.

I feel tense and walk towards the bridge hoping that Liesel will be there.

I've learned something from Allen and that is money is everything. It's everything because you can get a house and call the shots. When you're dressed properly grown-ups give you a bit of respect. But as long as I'm me and have no home and wear tattered clothes Allen will never give me proper clothes because that would mean that I can look like him. And no one who knows Allen looks like him. He makes sure of that. Even if it means he strips you himself. He always has to outdress you, outsmart you. It's his way. It's the grown-up way. He only wears Nike shoes and expensive jeans and tops. He always gives me clothes that are just about to fall apart, so that I'm always dependent on him. So that I will always go back to him for more and spend my money on him. But I understand. I have to do it. It's the only way I can be safe on the streets. There are too many monsters out there.

4

I get to the bridge and find that Liesel is not there. So I hang around Ma Zakes' spaza shop with Sealy. He buys me mageu and rolls a joint.

"Keep an eye out for the pigs," he says.

"Sure."

"Where were you last night?"

"Why?"

"Gerald fucked up this one guy with a goni because he called him driver as he got into his cab."

"Who was that stupid naai?"

"Liesel's outie. You checked him. He thinks he's hard because he's in Hard Livings."

"Ja, I know him. He's a real poes."

"I checked you like Liesel."

"What do you mean?"

"Don't give me that shit. You only buy your stop from her."

"Ja, because she doesn't make me wait like you ouens."

"Ag voetsek, you just want to naai her."

"It's not like that."

"Ay but you're full of kak. You never know what's going inside your head."

He lights up the joint and takes a long drag. TKZee belt out "Shibobo" from Ma Zakes'. I take a sip of mageu and let it settle at the back of my throat. Sealy bobs his head in rhythm. He's a bastard on the dance floor. He can outdance anyone and he's got style. That's why Gerald likes him. Gerald comes in with his white Ford Grenada. He makes a lot of noise before he parks it outside his shack not far from where we are sitting.

"Away, Sealy," he shouts as he gets out of the car.

"Away, Gerald," Sealy says and gets up to dance. I watch him from the bench, his feet shuffling pantsula-style, a cool sleepy look on his face. Just before he goes to Gerald he gives me his joint and another stop.

"Swaai us another pilletjie, ek sê."

I pull hard from the joint till it burns my fingers and kill it. "Shibobo" melts into another song by TKZee but I forget its name. I take another large sip of mageu but leave some for Sealy. He disappears into a shack with Gerald. I take my time smoking the zol, patiently waiting for Sealy. I end up smoking the whole zol. My thoughts are like water. I sit and listen to the chaos of the people living under the bridge. Everything just sounds deur-mekaar. A toddler walks up to me completely naked. She sits next to me on the bench and we look at each other for a while, a silly smile on my face.

"Jy! Trek aan jou klere!" Gerald yells and the toddler scurries away.

"What are you waiting for?" he says, standing over me. Sealy still hasn't come out of the room. But I notice a pigeon flying around Gerald's shack. The work of evil will never stop, I say to myself.

"Sealy," I say, a little nervous.

"Jy's dik geroek, nè?"

"Sorrie, ek bedoel Gerald."

"Jy, tsek jou naai, ek is nie 'n kaffir nie," he says and awakens my calm senses, with a fist across my face. I fall but pick myself up quickly and start running. I run out as quickly as I can. A few blocks away from the bridge I realise that I don't have my flip-flops. I wait at least five minutes before I go back. Gerald is nowhere in sight but his car is there. I take my strops and run. "Jy, jy!" I hear him behind me but I keep running. Once far from the bridge I slow down and calm myself.

I feel thirsty and go to a public toilet on Bree Street. A security guard who works near the open parking lot looks at me funny, like I'm a thief or something. But he leaves me alone. At the basin I pour water over my face as it is boiling hot and drink till my stomach swells and I burp. I sigh and feel my high returning. The air is so hot it feels like breathing in a carpet. I take another large sip, this time listening to my throat swallowing mouthfuls of fresh water. Water, I love water, I say looking at myself in the mirror. But I can never look at myself too long in the mirror as my blue eyes remind me of the confusing messages they send out to people. I wear my blue eyes with fear because fear is deeper than shame. I see a large shadow moving towards the entrance of the toilet. I make my way out only to find the security guard and a Rottweiler on a loose leash. But I have a secret and that is I have a way with dogs. Ever since I was bitten by a dog when I was seven, dogs have never bothered me again. He flicks the dog leash but nothing happens. I don't say anything. I just walk away.

I drift around town going to the station, the library, even taking a nap in the Gardens. I think of nothing but just enjoy my high. Fat pigeons that might be thugs or dirty politicians fly above me as I lie on the grass. Clouds form different shapes and disappear into the hot air. I could use another stop for tonight but I can't go back to Gerald empty-handed.

I walk back to Sea Point, the air thick with the smell of sea water.

5

The last couple of days have been difficult. I can't get a trick. No money means I can't see Allen and I can't go anywhere near the bridge. I walk around Sea Point nervously, keeping an eye out for Gerald's white Grenada. And I can't go to the bank because the bank has rules. Joyce said you can only take out your money on special days, not on weekends and you must give them a reason why you need the money, exactly like gangsters work. These clever gangsters that wear Italian suits, they are full of kak. Grown-ups are the same everywhere. They always want to control everything. All I want is a decent pair of shoes, to make up with Gerald and a Malawi stop to make me think I'm flying. Is that so much to ask for?

"Hey!" Bafana jumps at me from nowhere. I'm sitting near the Men's toilet at the beach.

"Fuck off!" I yell, holding my heart with my teeth. He laughs but stops when he sees how serious I am.

"I got a surprise for you."

"What are you talking about? Since when do you give me anything?"

"Just go with me, bra. I know what I'm doing."

"Look, I'm tired. I'm not walking to town and the sun is

about to go down. Just leave me alone. I've got enough to worry about."

"I promise, bra. We're not going far. Just further up the beach. Sunset Beach, that's where we're going. It's not far."

"What is this about, first? I'm not getting in trouble with cops for you."

"No. Nothing like that."

"Then what?"

"Just come with me, bra. I'm asking you nicely."

I get up reluctantly and follow him to Sunset Beach. He introduces me to two white kids who look older than us and have long noses. They look rich and bored with their money.

"Ja, so what do you want?" I say to the taller one.

"Aggression. Cool. I can get into that totally, man."

"Bra, don't speak to them like that. They're my friends."

"Shut up, Bafana. These are not your friends. Look at how you're dressed and look at how they're dressed."

"You two are cool, man. You know what I mean? Urban culture. Like urban living. You guys are living the concrete jungle, scavenging. Fuck, you don't need our help. Fuck, that would be an insult. You guys are like cats, urban cats. Survivors, man."

Bafana grins and nods his head while I listen to them. I make little sense of what they're saying.

"Yeah, so we were kind of trying to tap into your pool of

experience. Like we were wondering if you guys would be interested to trip with us."

"We've got good acid," the other says, "and we'll like feed you for the evening but it must be like a totally outdoor experience. Like we were wondering if you would take us to all of your hang-out spots at night. You know, to get the whole experience unedited."

"What are you saying? You want me to take drugs with you?"

"I'm in," Bafana butts in.

"Shuddup you," I tell him.

"Okay, you guys have got this aggression thing completely going. Is that like your way, like that survival of the fittest thing? Okay, I can see that. I can tap into that if you want."

"Look, I'm not taking drugs with you," I tell them.

"But this is going to be a totally awesome experience. Like don't you wanna tap into some raw energy? I mean, just think of it. Think of us making art, man. Right here right now," the shorter one says.

"What are you talking about? I'm hungry. I don't want to talk kak with you."

"Bra, they said they'll feed us," Bafana says.

"And then what?" I ask them.

"And then we'll have a totally awesome trip."

I start walking towards the park. Bafana comes after me.

"Fuck off, you poes. Your naai. If you want to take drugs fuck off," I say and curl my fist at him.

He lets me go. I hear him mumbling with the other two something about another guy Bafana knows about. They walk towards the Seven Eleven where the lights are always on.

I walk towards the Broken Bath, my strops making flapping sounds that irritate me. I take them off and put them in my jacket pocket. I walk on the beach and feel broken shells under my feet. They make a crackling sound which makes me sad. I hate sadness because it means tears are not far off. And I can't have that. Men don't cry. When have I ever seen Allen cry? Never. Or Gerald? Never. Or Sealy? And since I'm nearly thirteen I mustn't cry. I must be strong. I must be a man. That is what men do. They don't cry because tears are messy. They make your eyes all puffy and snot just runs from your nose and that's messy. Grown-ups aren't messy. They are always neat. They are neat because they don't cry. When does anyone see a grown-up walking in the street crying? Never. Even my father never cried. And my mother, she never cried. Her tears were her blood. She cried only when Papa beat her until she bled.

My stomach moans something awful as I walk along the beach. I go to the bins and have a scratch around. There is nothing but empty packets and drops of cool drink left in tins. Two men who look like hobos watch me closely as I scratch near their bin. They are drinking something.

"Hungry?" one of them says.

I go up to them. Sitting in the shadow of a spotlight the one stands up to shake my hand.

"What's your name?"

"Azure."

"Sit down."

I sit next to them but not on their blanket.

"Have a drink," the other offers me a half-empty two-litre bottle of cheap wine. I take a slug.

"Here, sit against the wall. It's still warm from the sun. It was hot today, huh?"

"Ja, it was hot."

We drink like that for a while. The other's stomach also moans. He coughs and spits out a blob of green from his throat. It's obvious that they also have no bread. But I sit with them even though I don't drink much wine. White wine or any wine for that matter always makes my head spin.

"Don't drink much, do you?" the one who asked me over says. "By the way I'm David and this is Pieter."

I can hear that they're both Afrikaans but I don't attempt to speak their language. That's how grown-ups fuck you. If you're too eager to please, to say hi and make a friend they think you're a moegoe and take you for a ride.

"It's going to be warm tonight," I offer.

"We'll sleep well," Pieter says.

27

"Not if you snore," David says.

"Ag, los my uit, man. Ek is moeg."

"Praat jy Afrikaans?" Pieter asks.

I shake my head.

"Engelsman, nè?"

"Sotho," I say.

"Joburg," David says.

"Ja."

"I thought so. You don't find many Sotho mense in Cape Town. All the darkies speak Xhosa here."

A huge wave comes crashing on the rocks. We keep quiet and drink the wine.

"You don't drink much," he says again. I take a large sip.

"I get a headache if I drink too much."

"Babelas," Pieter says and laughs. He ends up coughing again and spits out another big blob of green.

"David, ek kan nie meer drink nie. My maag is seer, man."

Me and David polish off the bottle.

"Is jy honger?" he asks after a while.

I shake my head.

"Is jy dronk?"

I nod and burp.

"Jy's ôraait nou. Ek is ook van daai kant. Daai Vaalie mense, ek verstaan hulle nie."

I get up and stumble.

"Fifty bucks. Don't worry about that. What if I said I wanted to fuck you in my car?"

"You can do that too if you want."

"Of course I want."

We go to his car. His ring shimmers in the night.

"Do you always wear your wedding ring?" I say just so that he doesn't take me for a fool and try and cheat me after the sex.

"If I give you sixty will you shut up?"

"I can do that. I can be quiet."

The married ones are always the horniest and by far the roughest. He takes me in his family minibus to a dark beach near the V&A Waterfront. We are the only ones parked there. He takes me to the back seat and oils me with cooking oil before he takes me like a beast. I bite the seat in front of me while he grunts and moans. He goes at it at least for an hour before he comes into a condom. As soon as he is done he zips up his pants and takes out his wallet.

"It's your lucky day. I've only got two twenties and a fifty."

My face lights up even though my asshole is sore.

"Oh, but I've got coins," he says. He couldn't resist getting me back after I said he was married. Me and my mouth; I'm always on guard. He gives me a fifty-rand note and two five-rand coins.

"Do you want to do this again?" I ask.

"Maybe."

"Well, I'm always at the park at night."

"Great. It's been a slice of heaven but now I have to go," he says and opens the door for me to get out. He gets into the front seat and drives off. I walk towards the water and take off my pants. I sit in a shallow pool and let the cool water cover me up to my waist. I sit for a while until my bum feels numb.

7

I find Allen sitting at his usual place near the white girl. She's got stitches under her left eye and you can still see some bruises if you look past her flashy make-up. I'm nervous because I didn't see him three days later like he said and because he is wearing his dark RayBans. That means he's either stoned on drugs, got an ugly bruise or that he is in a foul mood. I go up to him anyhow.

"Allen, can I sit?"

"What the fuck do you want?"

"You said I can . . ."

"I say a lot of things. Do you always listen to everything I say?"

"Yes, Allen."

"And that's why you're on the streets and I'm here. Stupid fuck, just grow up."

"But I thought . . ."

"Did you really think I was going to get you shoes, mother-fucker?"

I don't answer.

"What, do I look like your mother?"

I shake my head.

"Listen, if you want to buy a TV or a hi-fi or something pricey I can get it for you at a hot price. But shoes, clothes, don't fuck with me. Understand?"

"Yes, Allen."

"See how I'm dressed?"

"Yes, Allen."

"No. Really see. RayBan. Gucci, Armani and Nike," he says pointing to his clothes.

I nod nervously.

"Now look at how you're dressed and compare it to how I'm dressed. Fuck, you stink. Now fuck off. I'm not the Salvation Army."

I get up and walk away quickly.

I walk towards town, all the time praying that Gerald and his rats won't see me. I go to Long Street to a shop called Second Time Around. They sell good second-hand clothing. And the woman who works behind the till is not a vulture. She lets you roam around for a while and get what you want, no matter how you look. I spot a pair of veldskoene that look like my size. I take them to the till even though the price sticker says sixty-five.

"I need these shoes," I say to her politely.

"How much have you got?"

"Sixty," I plead and take out the money.

She looks at me out of glasses that sit nearly at the bottom of her nose.

"Okay."

I give her the money. She rings it up on one of those old tills that make a lot of noise, like a toy.

"Thank you," I say, relieved.

I take off my strops and put them in my jacket. I put on the shoes anxiously. She watches me.

"Here," she says.

I stand up. A pair of socks is on the table.

"I don't have any money."

"I know. Take them," she says.

I take the socks and unfasten my laces. My dry feet make crackling sounds as I slide the socks over them. I tie the shoes properly.

"I can walk forever in these shoes," I tell her. "Thank you," I say and leave.

I can feel her eyes on me as I walk out of her shop. I go to Bree Street, not far from the mosque. I know a guy called Vincent who usually hangs around there. At night he sleeps outside one of the shops. He's also from Joburg.

"Mpintshi, I haven't seen you for a while," he says when he sees me.

"I'm in Sea Point now. Town's too rough for me."

"This is where all the action is. You know me, I like big cities."

"Ja, but Cape Town? Come on."

"It's better than Sea Point. You have to put up with all those gangsters," he says. He's older than me.

"Nah. I stay away from them."

"What's with the shoes, bra?"

"Hey, I needed shoes, they were the only ones I could get."

"I could have got you shoes, you know that."

"Ja, but there's Allen to think about."

"Oh him, I forgot. Is he still terrorising the neighbour-hood?"

"Ja, it's his neighbourhood. I have to go through him first."

We sit under a palm tree. He opens a pack of fish and chips and breaks half a loaf of white bread into two. We eat silently and finish the meal in no time.

"Ta, bra," I say to him.

"I've got to be straight with you, man."

"What?"

"The word is out on the street that Gerald wants you."

"Are you serious?" I say, terrified.

He just looks at me.

"Shit," I say.

"What did you do?"

"Nothing."

"What do you mean 'nothing'?"

"Nothing. I mean just that. Okay I was smoking a zol with Sealy and then Sealy left to do some shit with Gerald. So then

Gerald comes over to me and by mistake I call him Sealy. That's what happened."

"Fuck, you know how that nigger hates black people. You insulted him."

"Ja, but I didn't mean to. For fuck's sake it was a mistake. Shit. Now he's gonna moer me for it."

"Listen, stop hiding, 'cause he's been looking for you. Just go to him and say you're sorry and that you'll do anything he wants."

"Fuck."

"Got any money?"

"No, I just spent it on these shoes."

"It would have made it easier if you had some money."

"I doubt it."

"Don't worry, bra, you'll live through it. He won't kill you. See this railway line here," he says pointing to an old scar, eight stitches that run down the side of his head.

"Ja."

"Gerald gave me that. Look, don't even think of running away. Believe me, you won't get far. The man's got wheels. He'll fuck you up and kill you if you do that."

I breathe hard.

"I know you're scared, bra, but just go. But take off those shoes. You know Gerald, he's fucked up. He thinks he's white because he's got straight hair and a light skin. If you show up with those shoes and your blue eyes, he'll kill you. He'll say, Who the fuck do you think you are? Trying to be white?"

"But I'm not."

"I know that, bra. We come from Mshenguville together. I know that. But that asshole doesn't. He'd love to have your blue eyes. Everyone knows that except you. You must try and work around you, blue eyes."

"What do you mean?"

"I mean you have to be the blackest person."

"But I am dark. Look at my skin. I'm not far from makwere-kwere."

"No, I mean you have to be more black . . . like more black than all of us. You must watch what you wear. Like those shoes. Things like that give you away. Like if people see you and they don't know you're right, the first thing they look at is how you look. Right?"

"Right."

"So now they look at your blue eyes and your shoes and they think blue eyes, veldskoene, he's trying to be white. That's how people think. See what I mean?"

"Shit. I think I do."

"That's why people have beat you up all your life. They think you're not black enough."

"So what do I do? Why does everything have to be so hard?"

"Fuck, don't panic on me. I'm helping you. Just watch what you wear. Look at makwerekwere. Try and be a little more like them."

"Okay," I say pulling myself together.

"Maybe you must buy one of their tops."

"Are you mad? Allen will kill me. He'll fuck me up. He'll say, who are you trying to be? and I won't know what to say. Fuck no. But I'll make a plan."

"Take off your shoes," he tells me. "I know a guy who knows another guy. I'm sure we can get you other shoes. I'll sell these at one of the second-hand shops."

"Don't go to the one in Long Street."

"Which one?"

"You know the one near Mama Africa, the one with the nice woman who works there. That's where I bought them."

"Ja, I know the one you're talking about. No, keep the socks," he tells me.

I take out my strops from my jacket.

"These are the things Allen gave me."

"Ja, Allen. I'm not surprised. Did he shit you out?"

"Always."

"He's another bastard who thinks he's white."

"I thought he was white."

"No, you can see it in his eyes. I know he looks white but if you look at him closely you can see some coloured blood. He hates it, that's why he's so fucked up. I mean, imagine being nearly white but not quite. Know what I mean?"

"Mmm."

"That's why he's such an asshole."

"Ever seen him beat up one of his chicks? The other day he completely fucked up this white bitch who couldn't keep her mouth shut."

"Ja, but there's more to it than that. It's that white thing. It just eats him up that he's not all white. Why do you think he's always so well dressed?"

"I see what you mean."

"Check."

"Grown-ups are fucked up."

"No, Cape Town is fucked up. Really."

"You're right, it's Cape Town, not the people."

"And the people. Don't forget about the people. They're also fucked up."

"And now I must face them," I sigh.

"Look, you better go. It's best if you hand yourself in. Know what I mean?"

"If he catches me first . . ."

"Fuck knows what he'll do to you."

"Remember how my eyes used to get me in trouble at school?"

"Ay, they used to moer you at school."

"Nothing changes."

I chew my nails.

"Come back in a couple of days' time."

"If I'm still walking."

"Don't be so negative. Who knows, you might live to laugh about this one day."

I look at him and say nothing. This is my life we're talking about, I think.

"Anyway, come back in a couple of days' time and I'll have shoes for you."

8

The first person I go to look up under the bridge is Liesel. I stand outside her shack while she looks at me.

"Where have you been?"

I say nothing but keep looking at her.

"He's looking for you. You better go now," she says and disappears back into her room.

I walk nervously towards Gerald's shack. I see his white car parked outside his room. Someone is washing it. Sunlight from between the two highways cuts the road underneath in two. I walk in the middle of the light. Ma Zakes' is open. I can hear TKZee belting out a song. Sealy is sitting on the bench. He sees me but says nothing. I know what I have to do. I walk up to him and ask him if he has seen Gerald. He punches me across the face. I fall down in utter shock.

"Sorry, I have to do this," he says, "he's watching."

He kicks me in the ribs as I'm about to get up. The sun is hot, hot.

"Get up," he tells me.

I get up, holding my broken ribs. He punches me again with a strong left hook. I stagger and land on my face. He kicks me in the head and stamps on it, grinding me into the tar road. I start screaming and grab his leg. He fucks up my face with his fists. My nose starts bleeding and snot runs. "Sealy, I'm sorry," I beg. He continues hitting me. Eventually I let go of his leg and roll up into a ball to protect my head. He kicks my back and rips off my jacket. The music plays on. The sun beats.

"That's enough." I hear Gerald's voice. He walks dancing to the beat of TKZee.

Sealy walks away. I sit up as I can't stand up immediately.

"What did you think you were doing? Did you think you could just say anything to me and get away with it?" he says, towering over me.

One of Gerald's sluts is beside him. She wears a tight short dress that shows off her loose thighs.

"Moer him," she says, "he doesn't respect you."

I cower away and wait for the next blow but it doesn't come.

"Get up," he says, almost tenderly.

I cover my face as I get up.

"I'm not going to dirty my hands on a piece of shit like you."

"I'm sorry, Gerald," I say and two teeth fall out.

"You see that car?"

"Yes, Gerald."

"Clean it and polish it nicely. When I'm satisfied you can clean up."

I limp towards the car. One of my eyes is completely shut. Underneath the other eye is a bad cut. I just let the blood flow.

"And don't you fucking get any blood near my car," he says and throws my torn jacket at me.

I take it and wrap it around my waist. The guy who was cleaning the car tells me to only polish the car as it has already been washed.

"Hey, jou naai! Polish it slowly and do it properly," he orders me. To mock me he opens his mouth wide and flashes his tongue between a gap in his front teeth.

The music from Ma Zakes plays louder.

"Where can I get polish?" I ask swallowing blood.

He points to Gerald's room. I stand at the door and wait.

"What do you want?" a coloured woman shouts at me. Behind her I can see broken shoes stacked on a rack towards the roof. They look like trophies. I spot my old shoes and hope that Gerald won't turn me into a rat or a pigeon.

"Polish for Gerald's car."

"I don't have it here. Ask Gerald. Now voetsek," she says and closes the door in my face.

I limp to Gerald. He sits on the bench and talks to Sealy and the other rats.

"Tsek! Tsek!" one of them gets up and waves his arm at me.

"Los hom," Gerald says.

"Jy. Wat soek jy?" Sealy asks.

"Polish for the car."

"Tell this poes I didn't ask him to polish my car," Gerald says to Sealy. I'm confused but keep silent. I'm sure he said, Clean and then polish my car.

"Do you want another one?" Sealy says and gets up. He smacks me across the face with a hot klap. Strangely, I remain standing. My face is numb with pain.

"Hey, jou naai." Gerald kicks me. "I said, clean my car, not polish it."

The police drive in. A few squatters in the back scatter to their rooms. The cops drive slowly towards us. Gerald remains calm. The car stops near us. I stand with my back to them. If I'm smart I'll stay like this till they leave, I tell myself. Gerald gets up to talk to one of the officers. They speak quickly before the car drives off again.

"Hey, jou poes, I'm not finished with you," Gerald says.

I try to remain still but my head sways.

"Clean my tyres with your spit," he says.

"What are you still doing here? Fuck off," Sealy says and kicks me in the ribs. I fall but manage to pick myself up again. I untie the jacket round my waist and spit into it. With my blood and spit I clean the tyres.

"Don't touch my mag wheels, jou naai, poes," Gerald shouts.

I do it slowly but every time Sealy walks nearby I work faster.

"This poes is finished," Sealy says after a while. He grabs me by the scruff and drops me near the garbage bins.

"Wait there," Gerald says.

I remain standing even though my head feels dizzy. Gerald calls for someone on his cellphone. Not long after a brown Ford Cortina pulls in and parks near Gerald and the boys. Two men wearing shiny tracksuits that I've never seen anywhere else come out of the car. They greet each other like the gangsters they are. Soon one of them grabs me by my shirt and bundles me into the car. They take me to Somerset Hospital.

One of the gangsters called Richard stays near me. They call me into the examining room. Richard looks at me as if he's about to spit in my face but he doesn't. If you're wise, act like you're not that sick, I tell myself. Richard follows me into the white room where the doctor is and closes the door behind him.

"What happened?" the white doctor asks.

"They caught him stealing at a shop. The manager fucked . . . I mean beat him up. We watched the whole thing happening so we brought him here. He's lucky that we were there. He nearly killed him. He was about to get his gun."

"Trouble with these kids is that you don't know what to do with them," the doctor says writing down something.

"Ja, they are just problems. People talk about crime. These kids are crime," Richard says.

"And they won't go to school or a home. They spend their lives sniffing glue and smoking buttons."

Richard says nothing.

"Right, put this on," the doctor says and hands me a blue dress for patients.

I take off my clothes and stand there naked. I don't bother with the blue dress. He points to a white bed and asks me to sit there.

"You better put this around your waist, this is not a jungle," he says. "I'm getting a nurse to clean up your face first."

I wrap the blue dress around my waist like a towel. He closes a white curtain around me and tells Richard that he can wait outside. We'll be a while, he says.

The doctor returns with an Indian nurse. He fiddles in the room with his medical things while the nurse cleans my face with swabs of cotton.

"What happened?" she asks.

I say nothing.

"This is going to sting," she says as she cleans the cut under my left eye.

"Right, I'm ready," the doctor says and returns carrying a tray with silver instruments.

"With the trouble he's been causing I have a good mind not to use a local anaesthetic," he says and injects something near my eye.

"What's he been up to?" the nurse asks, still swabbing me.

"Caught stealing. Apparently the manager did this to him. Don't blame him though. He was probably just trying to run an honest business till trouble came along."

The nurse keeps quiet.

"How old is he? Probably thirteen, fourteen. Ran away from home. They all do, you know. Wild kids. And now he's caught stealing a bar of chocolate or something pathetic like that. He deserves what he got," he says sewing up my cheek.

The nurse looks into my eye and says nothing.

"Hold still," he says impatiently.

"I feel dizzy." I open my mouth and a little blood splatters on his white coat.

"I'm nearly done. Just hold still for a little while. Problem with these kids is that they want everything now. They won't wait for anything. Have you seen how they harass you in town begging you for money after they nearly make you crash into the car you are supposed to park behind? I don't trust them. And I never give them money. What for? So that they can buy drugs."

She listens but doesn't nod.

"Right, I'm done. Give him something to settle that dizziness. I'm just going to clean up."

The nurse gives me something to gargle and stop my gums from bleeding. She watches me struggle to the basin to spit out the salty stuff she gave me.

"What's wrong with your leg? Where does it hurt?"

"My ankle," I tell her.

"Don't worry, we'll take an X-ray."

The doctor returns in a clean coat. He prods my ribs and watches my face for reactions. I wince as little as I can. He also prods my back.

"Your back is black and blue with bruises. Nothing a few days' rest won't heal. I hope you've learned your lesson."

"He's been complaining about this ankle, doctor."

"I know, nurse. Take him to Dr Michael in Orthopaedics. I'm done with him," he says and writes something in a folder. He gives the nurse the folder and leaves. She cleans my other eye and puts a patch over it.

"Where are your clothes?" she asks.

"Over there," I say and point to a corner.

"Don't get up," she says, "your ankle is swollen."

She gives me my clothes and strops and closes the curtain. I hear her open and close the door. I dress slowly and put on my strops. Then I limp to the basin again and look at myself in the mirror. All I see is purple, red and a little blue staring back. My face is swollen. I can hardly tell that it's me looking back. The door opens and the nurse returns with a wheelchair.

"Thanks," I say looking at her shyly from the corner of my good eye.

She wheels me down the corridor. We pass Richard and his mate and go into a lift. At Orthopaedics Dr Michael takes two X-rays and looks at them from a light on the wall. He tells me that I have a fractured ankle but that it is not severe.

He writes something in the folder and then the nurse wheels me into another room where they put wet plaster around my ankle and foot. The plaster goes halfway up my shin. The nurse lets me try a few crutches before I choose the one which feels right. She gives me painkillers and wheels me back to Richard and his mate.

"Keep well," she says as I limp out the door. "Don't forget to come back in about eight days' time to take out the stitches."

Once inside the car Richards says, "Hey, gemors, they moered you nè? Poes, I hope you learned your lesson." He takes my painkillers.

"I can get off here," I say once we're outside the gates. "I don't live far from here."

"Where do you think you're going? Gerald isn't finished with you."

My heart sinks. We drive past Sea Point and Green Point and head towards town. We drive past the train station and go towards Woodstock. We stop outside a house in Salt River.

"Leave that in there, you won't be needing it," Richard says when I reach for my crutch.

I limp towards the gate. Richard goes first, then his mate. I follow behind. A woman wearing hot pants greets us at the door. She speaks in Afrikaans with Richard. They lead me through the building. Other girls pass by. I see an Indian man coming out one of the many rooms fastening his belt hastily.

He doesn't look at us as we walk past him. Outside there is a small room tucked away in the corner near the washing line. Richard opens the door and tells me to go inside. I step into the room. He closes the door behind me and locks it.

9

For three days they don't open the room. I shit in a toilet bowl they left in the room for me. My bed is just a sponge. For three nights I listen to my wounds, my bruises. For three nights I feel my body healing. On one wall is a mirror and on the other wall a light switch. At night when I'm bored, I play with it and watch the mirror. When the light goes off the mirror seems to suck in the light. I'm getting stronger, I tell myself, even though my stomach grumbles. When I start to feel weak, I sing. Made-up songs that have nothing to do with words, just non-sense sounds that keep writing themselves in my head. Some-times I just hum one note and see how long I can hold it. I do that for a long time. I'm getting stronger, I tell myself again and feel my stomach muscles forming in hard ridges. Destroy, destroy, the music plays on in my head.

I lie on my back and stare at the light till I see half-circles of fire. Then I turn off the lights and destroy the room with half-circles of fire. A volcano rages in my head as I do this. When the fire starts fading I turn on the lights again and stare at the light. I do this for most of the night and sleep during the day. You're getting stronger, I tell myself and turn off the lights. I start to feed off the light and begin to slowly forget my hunger.

Grown-ups, this is how they teach me to be strong. I take in their light and destroy them with fire.

When I was a child I used to like playing with matches. I used to strike a match and watch the fire burn the little stick until it was black. It was amazing to watch this. I used to steal the matches from my mother's secret hiding place and play outside behind the shack. I always felt guilty so I only used a few matchsticks because mother needed them to light candles. Once, when I was small, I can't remember how small but I remember that I still used to sleep in the same bed with my parents, I burned the bed by mistake. I was playing with matches and somehow the bed caught on fire. I tried to put it out. I remember using my spit but the fire had its own mind. It wouldn't listen. So I ran outside and called my parents who were talking with one of our neighbours. I remember my parents never beat me for that. They were too scared that they had left out matches for me to find and for me to play with.

My mother cried that day. She sat outside the shack and cried while my father tried to put out the flames. I think she cried because I was a naughty child. I always remember that day when things get hard. I remember how we had to sleep on the floor because I burned the bed. Not once did they hit me. Not once. And that was very strange because my father used to hit me for everything I did that he didn't like. And that was a lot. But for the fire he never touched me.

* * *

It is Richard who opens the door. He finds me sleeping.

"Hey, gemors, wake up!" he yells and bangs the door. He stands like a shadow at the door. You're blocking the light, I say to myself. As if he reads my mind he comes towards me and kicks my cast. I get up at once and stand. "You think you're strong, nè?" he says and pushes me. I fall on the sponge and remain there. "Get up, I've got no time for games, you poes."

I put on my T-shirt and wrap my torn jacket round my waist. "Take your shit and empty it outside, it stinks in here."

I go outside and empty the toilet bowl into the toilet outside.

"Did you flush, gemors?"

"Yes, Richard."

"Everything?"

"Yes, Richard, everything."

"And you stink too. Go inside!" he says and pushes me again.

I nearly fall as it is not easy to walk with a cast. At the kitchen door one of the girls gives me Lifebuoy soap and a little rag. She gives me a large plastic dish and tells me to go outside.

"Wash," Richard tells me and points to a tap outside.

I fill the orange dish with water and put it on the ground. Then I take off my clothes. When I look at my reflection in the water I notice that the eye patch has fallen away and that my bad eye is beginning to open up slowly. I splash my face with water first. The swelling has gone down. The girl stands at the door and watches me. I stand with one foot, the one without the cast, in the water. First I soak the rag before I put soap on it. When bubbles start to appear I slide the rag first over my bad leg up to my knee.

"You must wash everything, you hear? I want you clean."

"Yes, Richard."

"Even your ballas," the girl says and giggles stupidly.

I wash while they watch me. The sun is setting. Clouds start burning with fiery orange. I wash quickly and dry myself with the little rag. When I'm done I pour the water into a drain.

"Right, let's go," Richard says. He walks behind me as we go through the house. In one room I see the girls watching TV. I look quickly and concentrate on walking as Richard is behind me. I get in the back seat. We drive towards town.

We get off in a coloured area and go towards a block of flats. The lift is broken so we use the stairs. Richard lets me walk in front. I hang on to the banister as I walk. It's a noisy block of flats. Children run everywhere and the lights aren't working on all the floors. And it stinks of piss and shit. In one corridor a fire burns in a tin drum. Some of the people look like bergies. We walk past them and past the writing on the wall. "Mandela se poes," Richard reads out loud the writing on the wall when we reach the top floor. He says it like it's a doorbell message, like it's something he says every time he gets there. I stand back as he unlocks the door.

"You're not going in there," he says and lets his mate in. He opens another door near the flat. I go up a little staircase in the dark. Richard puts on his lighter and unlocks the door. He pushes me onto the roof and locks the door behind me.

From where I'm standing I can see the city. I can see the library, the train station, even the Cape Sun with its golden light. I put on my torn jacket and sit against the warm wall. My stomach moans. Sshhh, I tell myself. You're getting stronger. I must repeat this to myself.

When it is dark and the moon is out Richard opens the door and gives me a loaf of white bread wrapped in newspaper and a pint of milk. I eat half a loaf and drink half of the milk. I save the rest for morning. About an hour later my stomach starts grumbling like something is cooking and boiling inside it. After a while I grab some newspaper and run towards one corner of the roof. I drop my pants and my bum explodes into a terrible fart, shit flying out in a soup. I go like that for most of the evening. I decide to eat the rest of the bread but stay away from the milk. Maybe tomorrow I'll be lucky and they'll let me go, I say but not with too much hope. I say it because that's what a grown-up would say if a grown-up was in my shoes. Maybe tomorrow, I repeat and hold my asshole tight.

I sleep well because I'm outside and the air is warm. When I breathe in I can smell the sea.

* * *

In the morning, before sunrise, Richard opens the door and leaves out a plate of chicken, a whole chicken. I eat all of it and feel very thirsty afterwards. I look at the milk but I don't drink it. I explore the roof and watch people below. I watch them getting into their cars and getting out of their flats. I watch children running down the street playing soccer. I watch pigeons, ugly fat pigeons, flying around me endlessly and settling on the roof. Some of them only have one leg. And the men pigeons are always trying to screw the women pigeons. They bully them and hop on their backs. They are not very nice to look at, the men pigeons. They look fat and have this heavy throat that just hangs like an extra piece of meat. Every time they get on the roof I scare them away. But it's no fun scaring them one at a time. You have to wait. You have to wait till they all gather, maybe twenty of them. And then you just get up suddenly and run towards them. They make a nice sound when they fly away.

I get very thirsty so I stop running up and down. And there isn't any shade on the roof so I take off my T-shirt and sweat in the sun. The pigeons gather and watch me. They clean their wings and shit on the roof. They also make irritating noises that only pigeons make and the men ones as always run after the women ones. They'll do anything for a quick lay.

I'm about to fall asleep when a strange thing happens. Seagulls fly by. They make a lot of noise and terrorise the pigeons. I get up and watch the pigeons clumsily flying off, some of them falling over each other. I laugh when one seagull attacks a man pigeon. It isn't much of a fight. With its strong beak the seagull rips off some of the pigeon's feathers before the pigeon flies away. It takes only a few seagulls, nine of them, to scare away maybe thirty stupid pigeons. They are beautiful seagulls. They have white feathers that they look after and you never see a seagull that looks battered with dirty wings like some pigeons. Seagulls have pride, they always wash at sea with cold water. Like me. I watched the seagulls a lot when I first came to Cape Town. They're not stupid like pigeons. Pigeons are stupid because they let themselves get used. Where did anyone ever see a seagull being used as a messenger bird? Never.

The seagulls walk around the hot roof awkwardly, all the time crowing angrily. After a while the sun gets too much for them and they fly off somewhere. But they soon return if only to irritate the pigeons that start to gather. I forget my thirst when I look at them and think of swimming in the sea. I think of white waves crashing on the rocks and bubbles flying in salty air. I think of how sea water makes your skin dry if you don't rinse off at once. I think of Bafana and start to feel sad. Why is he outside and I'm up here? Why do I get into trouble and he doesn't even though he takes millions of drugs? And where are the police? Why are they never around when you need them? Why do they speak with people like Gerald? Why are they only interested in the big guy with the BMW who gets his car stolen in daylight? Why are they so scared of the night? Why don't they ever come out at night when you need them the most? Do they sleep well or are they also scared of bad things that come out at night?

The seagulls come back again and scare off the pigeons. After a while I start to feel sorry for the pigeons. They're not strong like seagulls. Some of them have one leg and bad rashes that leave them with patches of pink flesh where there were once feathers. But they're stupid for not living like seagulls.

Night comes and they still don't open for me. My mouth is dry with thirst. I look at the milk and find that it has gone off. With nothing to eat and nothing to drink I sit on one corner of the roof, my legs dangerously dangling over the ledge. Then the door opens.

"Gemors, what are you doing there?" Richard asks but stands at the door.

I get away from the ledge and walk towards him.

"Don't you want something to drink?" he asks.

"Yes, Richard."

"Come in then."

We go to his flat. Three other guys are in a room without chairs and a table. They sit on bean bags and watch a big TV. In the middle there is a silver tray with crushed buttons and zol and three bottlenecks. Richards gives me a plate of food and then goes to the tray.

"My sister made this breyani," he says. His eyes are not as aggressive as they usually are.

"Thanks, Richard," I say.

"Don't thank me, just eat."

I sit near the TV without getting in anyone's view. It plays a string of music videos. The others start smoking bottlenecks. I eat quickly and put back my plate at the sink. I take an empty jug from the sink and just fill it with water. I drink as much as I can without getting sick.

"Hey, gemors, you finished?"

"Yes, Richard."

"Was it nice?" he says, spaced out.

I nod my head.

"Come here," he calls me to one room. I follow him.

"This is where I sleep. You see?"

"Yes, Richard." His room is stuffy and a mess.

"Close the door."

I close the door. He opens his fly and lets out his piel.

"Come here."

I hesitate.

"Hey, gemors, don't make me shout. I just gave you nice food."

"Yes, Richard," I say and come close to him.

"Sit on the bed," he says.

I sit on the edge of his bed. He stands with his dick in my face.

"Tsek jou naai! Jy dink jy's mos 'n kleuring, nè? Suig. Suig," he says and shoves his dick in my mouth. "Open properly, jou naai. Poes. Tsek. Take it all in."

I do as I'm told. He stands there and starts rocking his pelvis. My jaws get tired. I take his dick out of my mouth and wank him.

"Tsek, jou naai! Suig. I know how to skommel."

I put it back in my mouth. The door opens.

"Hey, what's going on in here? I also want to join the party," one of them says and laughs. Richard smiles as the other unzips his fly.

"It's my turn," he says and shoves his semi-erect dick against my cheek.

"Tsek, Richard," he jokes.

Richard takes out his piel from my mouth but he doesn't put it away. He starts playing with himself while I suck the other's piel. Soon they all join in and take turns with my mouth. "Suig, suig," they keep prodding me. In my head I hear seagulls screeching violently, swooping over the sea as waves come crashing down. They are giving you their salt. I tell myself. Eat it, be strong. I start sweating. After a while my jaws become stiff but I continue sucking their smelly dicks with white stuff like pap on them. They make me give them blowjobs till they all come. At least they don't come in my mouth. They come all over my shirt. Afterwards they all sleep in various rooms. I go to the toilet and wash my T-shirt.

"Gemors," I hear Richard's voice, "where are you?"

I come out with my wet T-shirt and just look at him. He just looks back at me for a while and says, "You're sleeping outside again. It's too hot in here en julle kaffirs stink."

I follow him out the door and onto the roof. He locks the door behind me. I wait at the door till his footsteps fade. When I look out I see seagulls perched on the edge of the roof. They stand there like statues till one of them opens his wings and drops onto the warm roof. It's a man seagull. You can tell from the way he walks. The others stand there and wait. I also stand at the door and wait. He waddles towards me and stops about a kick away. Then he shits there and flies back to the others. Without thinking I walk over and put my finger into the mess. I scribble a cross on the door with it. They start crowing and flapping their wings. Then I walk to the mess and piss in it. I go back to the wall and sit there. They all fly towards the puddle in a mad rush and put their feet in it and then they all fly away except for the man seagull. He stands guard on the edge of the roof. I smile and close my eyes. I'm getting stronger, I whisper to myself before I fall asleep.

* * *

The next day Richard wakes me up after sunrise and tells me to get in the car with him and his mates. We drive in silence till we get to the bridge. Richard hands me my crutch as I get out of the car. Gerald is the first person I see from under the bridge. Everybody else is still sleeping except for the pigeons perched above the bridge. They croak and watch with beady eyes. I wait outside Gerald's shack while he talks in Afrikaans with Richard and his mates. Then they drive off. Gerald calls me over. The burglar bar at the door separates us.

"What's your name, Blue Eyes?" he finally says.

"Azure."

"What kind of a name is that, Blue Eyes?"

"My mother gave it to me."

"Then your mother was very stupid because how is any-one . . . how am I supposed to remember that name?"

I say nothing. I lean against the crutch for all the support I can get and look at the ground.

"You see, my name is very easy to remember, if you know me," he smiles. "Do you think you know me now, Blue Eyes?"

"Yes, Gerald."

"Good. So don't fuck with me again. I think we understand each other now, don't we, Blue Eyes?"

"Yes, Gerald."

"But your name we have to do something about it. Blue. Mmmh, blue. Blue. Blue, blue. You like it?"

"What?"

"Your new name."

"Yes, I like it, Gerald."

"What's your new name?"

I hesitate but say "Blue".

"You see, you're not that stupid."

He goes inside and fiddles in the back.

"You see, I'm not such a bad guy," he says and gives me my old shoes and a T-shirt with a lion print in front.

"Thank you, Gerald."

"Enough with that now. Just take it. If you're ever going to survive you better stop saying thank you, thank you. Are you stupid or something? Look at your face and your leg. You've got nothing to say thank you about. Okay. So fucking stop it or I'll moer you. Do you want me to moer you again?"

"No, Gerald."

"No, Gerald, that's better."

I nod my head. New lesson – no thank you, I say to myself. And No, Gerald. No Gerald! No, Gerald!

"Now just take off that fucking T-shirt," he says suddenly getting worked up, "and that jacket, Blue. You can't use it any more, it's finished."

I give him the old T-shirt with bloodstains and the jacket. The pigeons croak and one of them flies away. He gives me one shoe.

"I'll keep the other one for now," he says.

"Gerald?"

"Don't even ask. This is your new home. I own you now.

Who do you think paid for your hospital bills? Jy raak my ge-woond, nè? Tsek! Who fed you these last couple of days? Tell me who? Because I really want to know."

"You, Gerald," I say and look at the ground.

"That's right, me. So now I own you. Understand?"

I nod. It is too difficult to say Yes, Gerald to that. He walks to the mobile toilets and goes in. He stays there a while before he comes out again.

"Everybody has a job here. So go and do whatever it is that you do but just be back by five. I've got an important job for you. And Blue . . ."

He looks at me square in the eye.

"Don't disappoint me."

I nod my head and go.

10

I go to town near Subway. It is early. Few people walk the streets. I bump into Vincent working near my usual section.

"Where've you been? I heard about you," he says.

"Everywhere and nowhere really. What did you hear?"

"That Gerald moered you."

"Since when does Gerald moer anyone? He got Sealy to moer me."

"Oh, then you were lucky. If he moered you himself, he might have killed you. Know what I mean?"

"No."

"Gerald lives at the bridge and keeps a low profile for a reason."

"What?"

"But you can be such a laaitie sometimes."

"Look, I know he does drugs and everything."

"Fuck the drugs. Word is he killed some people. Well, let me say he killed a family. Two kids and the wife and husband."

"So why isn't he in jail?"

"Wait. He didn't just kill any family. Remember when the Staggies got killed?"

"Ja."

"Well. Gerald took out one of Staggie's powerful connections, bra. Out like that. One time, the whole family. You mustn't fuck with Gerald. He'll kill you."

"But the police. Why didn't they do anything?"

"Don't talk kak. What could they do? He did them a favour. He took out a powerful drug lord."

"Ja but still."

"Ja but still what? How can you say that? Which planet are you living in? This is South Africa, bra. The police were also in it. Times are shit. They also wanted a slice of the action. So you see you mustn't be a windgat with Gerald. He'll take you out. One time and no one will do anything about it. I mean fuck, you're just another street kid. Worse, you don't even have any connections in Cape Town except for me."

"So the police are also in it?"

"Of course. Ba Batla borotho. They want to eat well. Streets are hard, hey. We give those assholes a tough time. Half of them are fucked on crack and buttons when they go to work."

"So that's why I saw Gerald talking to the cops."

"He has to. He can blow their whole cover. So they give him breathing space under the bridge. That's his castle. Thing is the guy is loaded but he can't spend his money and he knows it. You know how that would fuck with anyone. I mean, imagine being worth a lot of money. I mean, I don't know how much money Gerald has. Maybe millions and he can't spend it because of the shit he's into. It fucks with you. Fuck, Gerald is a predator. Be very careful around him."

I take in the information and sigh.

"Don't worry, you'll be all right. Just don't fuck with him."

"But now, how come you are here and I'm in there?"

"Because there's only room for one predator at a time. Like in that movie *Jurassic Park*."

"I haven't seen it."

"You never saw *Jurassic Park*! What have you been doing in Sea Point?"

"Hiding. Anyway, you were saying about that movie."

"Ja, in that movie, right, there's this dinosaur. You know what that is, don't you?" he says laughing.

I nod my head. "I know what you're talking about. They were monsters as big as the Cape Sun that used to eat each other."

"Ja, those. Right. Now one of them was called T-rex."

A car drives near. The guy indicates to go in but decides to move off when he sees Vincent.

"Poes. Anyway, T-rex was king of the dinosaurs. He was like a lion. He killed them all. Everything. In this movie, right, they try to control T-rex but they can't. They put him in a cage but he manages to escape. In the end T-rex eats people, the guys who captured him. It's heavy. You see him chewing this one guy in half in one bite. Funny!"

"Why are you telling me this?"

"Mpintshi. You gotta learn to listen if you're ever going to survive."

"Right, I'm sorry. Go on."

"So now T-rex, right, he's Gerald. You check," he says in one breath.

"What?"

"Just listen to me. Listen to me. T-rex, he's Gerald. You check," he says and looks me in the eye.

"Okay."

"Not okay. That guy is heavy, he'll destroy you. People talk of the devil. The devil is nothing. I've seen him and he was nothing like T-rex. You say why am I out here and you in there? Because T-rex put me in here. You check. That guy is heavy, Mpintshi, heavy. He knows everything. You can't fuck with him."

"Are you fucking with my head? He sounds like Allen."

"Please, Allen! Gerald can destroy him with his breath."

"What are you telling me? What about all the things you were saying about Gerald before?"

"Just listen. Gerald is T-rex. Understand it. Overstand it. I don't care, just accept it, all right? Look, have I ever lied to you?"

"No."

"Now why would I say a thing like that if it wasn't true? You check?"

"He took my shirt . . . my shirt with the blood," I tell him.

"Really. Look, we're not going to get any work done today. Let's go."

We go towards the train station.

"Ha! You also got a railway line, I see." He smiles and pokes the stitches under my left eye.

"Five. It's not too bad."

He grabs my crutch and starts hopping around with it.

"I see you got your old shoes back."

"Ja, I have to go through Gerald first now."

"This is Cape Town, never forget that. Okay?"

I nod.

"I got you new shoes. Nice ones. Tackies. Reebok."

"Ja, whatever. I'll wait till this comes off first," I say and point to my cast.

"You look different."

"They fucked me up."

"No, I mean there's something different about you."

"What?"

"I don't know. Something in your eyes."

"What are you talking about? Now you're talking kak. Are you doing an Allen on me?"

We cross the street and go through the station. People walk in every direction.

"Wait. I know what it is," he says excitedly, like he won a prize. "You look older. That's it, you look older."

"I feel it," I say, strangely agreeing with him. "I feel thirteen."

"When's your birthday?"

"Soon."

"You mean you can't remember?"

I shake my head.

"Fuck it. Then today is your birthday. I'll get some zol. I know where we can get good Malawi. They even wrap it up in cobs, fresh from Malawi."

"Good," I tell him.

We buy some mnqusho and mageu from the taxi rank and sit outside the old Castle and eat. I eat quickly.

"So you were saying about T-rex?"

"What was I saying? Let me think. Right, you were saying he took your shirt with the blood."

"Ja, right."

"And he's probably got your other shoe."

"Right, bra. I wanted to talk to you about that. I saw other shoes in his room. He's got them stacked up on a shelf."

"T-rex, he's hungry. He's always hungry."

"What do you mean? What is that T-rex shit?"

"I mean T-rex is hungry."

"But who's T-rex?"

"Azure, this isn't hard, man. Shit, you think life is $1 + 1 = 2$. Well, it's not. People have been doing this shit for ages. Let me tell you something. If you've got enough voetsek in you and you know the right people, with a bit of money you can do anything. And that's what Gerald did. He's T-rex. He's fucking destruction. And the police know it."

"They do? How?"

"Because they're also into the same shit. No normal man can deal with the shit these guys put up with so they use anything they can get."

"Like T-rex?"

"No, not like T-rex. T-rex is a predator. He works on his own. That's why Gerald lives under the bridge. They have to control T-rex, otherwise . . ."

"Fucking destruction."

"You check."

I nod my head and sigh. "What does T-rex want with me?"

"Don't ever mention T-rex when you talk about Gerald."

"Why?"

"Why? You ask stupid questions sometimes, you know. You must ask questions that go somewhere. You see that bird over there?" he says and points to a bird pecking at something near us.

I don't say anything. I feel my throat tightening up with fear.

"That's right. He can hear us. So you see, don't fuck with Gerald, he'll destroy you."

"Let's get some zol," I say nervously. But I remember that I have to be back at five.

We both get up. The pigeon watches us.

"Wait. He said I must be back by five. He said something about some job that I had to do for him."

"Then don't smoke. You know how you get when you smoke, bra."

"Ja, I know. Shit!" I say and let out a scream. "My life is fucked. Things are never going to be the same again."

"Don't be so fucked. You don't know that."

"Ja, but Gerald knows everything."

"He does," he says flatly, "no jokes."

"And he gave me a name too. Blue."

"He gave me Vincent."

"It kind of suits you. You look like a Vincent with your railway line."

"Blue. It's different."

"I don't like it."

"Be careful what you say," he says and points to the pigeon, still pecking away. I don't know whether to believe him or to laugh.

"You make me scared when you say things like that."

"Well, it's the truth."

"Listen, bra . . ."

"You need to go. Relax. I know."

We hug like brothers and then we walk together towards the station.

"I'll see you around," I say and walk towards the Gardens. He watches me while I walk.

11

My feet are sore, they have walked too much. My eyes hurt. They have seen too much. And it never ends. It just keeps going. I can hear a clock ticking in my head. I can hear bicycle spokes running, a car speeding. Speeding very fast, screeching. That sound, it goes on forever. In the Gardens I lie on my back and look at the sun through the shade of a tree. I see blades of light and fall asleep.

I dream deeply. I always do. My dreams are fragile enough to make me wonder. When I wake up I can only feel the sun on my face. The shadow has moved. It's the sun. It does that to everything. It moves things.

I look at the tree's branches. They are reaching out to the sky, to the sun. Feed me, they plead. Trees are beautiful. They are dancers. They are graceful. And they have quiet spirits. If you sit quietly long enough, you can actually hear a leaf falling. That's how trees speak. They drop things. They lose things all the time, so that others may find them. They know how to give, trees.

Fuck knows how many things I've lost along the way. The way in Cape Town, it's a long road, winding. I'm always lost, that's why I hide out in Sea Point. Get it? "See Point." That's where my eyes are. That's where I can see the best. I miss Sea Point. And I know that I can never go back there.

The air is warm and smells sweet from all the flowers in the garden. Pigeons hover near me. I look at them dancing near a branch. I know what fear is. I know what it means to be scared, to be always on the lookout. I know what it means to hear your own heartbeat. It means you are on your own. The world is watching you but only you can hear the music. The mad music of bicycle spokes and speeding cars. I know what it feels like to hear your own fear beating in your ear. I know what it feels like to bite the insides of your mouth to control the fear. I know what it feels like to bite your nails till your fingertips are raw and sensitive to everything you touch. I know fear. And I hate it. I live with it every day. The streets, they are not safe. They are roads to hell, made of tar. Black tar. There are things watching us when we sleep. Terrifying things. In my dreams I see terrifying things; monsters that steal our breath. Sometimes when I wake up I'm just glad that I woke up and didn't fall asleep forever. Forever is a long time. What would I dream of forever? If I had a choice I would dream of swimming. Nothing else – just swimming in the sun all day.

I think of Gerald and my heart begins to race. How will I ever face him? Death would be easier. He frightens me. I look at the pigeons, the stupid pigeons, and wonder.

It's my birthday today. I'm thirteen. I feel it too, all those numbers. I can see them clearly and they all make thirteen. One. Three. I must understand that number. I must understand what it means to be a grown-up if I'm going to survive. That's what they all keep telling me. Grow up. Fast. Very fast. Lightning speed. Everything is always like that. Quick. You must act quickly. Understand quickly. Otherwise someone will fuck you up nicely. They'll beat you up so that you must always remember. When you go to the toilet and you feel a terrible pain in your stomach and balls, every time you sit you will remember that everything has to be quick. You will shit quickly because it hurts too much if you take your time. They will make sure you remember.

And you must do everything. You must because they say so. If they say Jump, you must jump. If they say Sit, you must sit. Otherwise they will fuck you up nicely. They always do if you don't do like they say. You must do like Gerald says, I tell myself.

I look at the sun directly and my eyes strain. When I look around me I see fire. I see lots of fire. You're getting stronger, I tell myself. No thank you, Gerald. No thank you. I must learn this. I must understand what it means. No thank you. The grown-ups want me to understand this. When I do I will survive. This is what they tell me. Even Vincent tells me this.

I've been walking around town like a lost dog all day. Everyone seems to know where they are going except me. I ask someone for the time and decide to go home. Blue, that's my new name. The bridge, that's my new home. Out here the world passes you by if you don't listen. It crushes you. Go home, I tell myself. You are getting stronger.

* * *

I go to the bridge. Gerald's car is outside his shack. I lean my crutch against one wall of his shack.

"I've been expecting you," he says when I go to the door. He opens the burglar door and lets me inside. "Sit on the bed," he tells me.

I try not to look around even though my mind is racing with curiosity. It is dark in his room. There are no windows.

"Drink," he says and offers me some cooldrink in a glass. "I'm glad that you came earlier than I expected you. Did you meet Vincent?"

"Yes," I confess.

"Good."

He walks to the corner of the room while I sit facing the door, the light. He gives me blue tracksuit pants. The material glitters.

"Put this on," he says.

I take off my pants nervously and put on the blue pants. He takes the old pants to the corner of the room. I hear him shuffling with some clothes behind me.

"You have learned to live with fear," he says.

I keep quiet. He closes the door and locks it. I'm scared. He lights a candle and puts it on the table facing the door. Then he pulls a chair beside me.

"Do you know who I am?" he says. He is wearing an orange T-shirt.

"You must never wear this colour," he tells me. "Only the sun and I can wear it. Understand, Blue?"

I nod my head.

"Why are you scared? And don't think about it."

"I am scared of the dark," I tell him.

"What's there to be scared of?"

"Monsters."

"Do you think I'm a monster?"

I don't answer him and he smiles.

"Do you know who you are?"

"I don't know anything anymore," I tell him.

"That's why you came to me," he says. "I brought you here. I stole you from your parents. I killed them."

I remember Vincent's words. Ask questions that go somewhere.

"I killed your parents because they were going to hurt you."

"But I loved my mother and she loved me."

"You didn't love your mother. You feared that she would say no to anything you did. You did everything to please her. Your father hated you for that. He was going to kill you."

My head feels dizzy as I take this in.

"You ask why, don't you?"

"Yes."

"Are you still thirsty?"

"I'm always thirsty."

He pours me a glass of water. I drink quickly.

"Your mother thought she was an angel. Her father loved her above all the other children. She gave you that thing. That's why people have been beating you up all your life."

I listen.

"You must let your mother go. At night when you sleep she calls you. You dream of her, don't you?"

"Always."

He pours himself some cooldrink from the same glass I used and puts it on the table, near the candle. I watch it bubble.

"Do you know who you are?" he asks again.

"No, Gerald, I don't."

He takes off his clothes and sits naked on the chair. The light catches part of his face and his tight muscles.

"Do you know who I am?"

"Yes, Gerald."

"Do you see what your mother has done to you? She has made you a puppet, a fool. You say yes to everything."

"No, Gerald," I say. Learn this, I tell myself.

He takes my left hand and points to a scar on the inside of my wrist.

"Do you know what this is?"

"No, Gerald."

He turns his back. A huge scar with horns runs down it. It seems alive in the candlelight.

"You burned me when you were three. Remember?"

"No, Gerald."

"You burned me with fire when you burned your bed. You gave me a sign. You wanted me to see you when the time came. You asked for me. Do you remember?"

"No."

"I stole your memories, the things you did to me. After you burned me you nearly gave me death with drugs."

"I want to ask something," I say nervously.

"Then ask it, damn it. Don't always wait for me."

"But I fear you. I fear that you will hit me."

"Your father used to beat you. Did you fear him?"

"No, Gerald."

"Do you see what your mother did to you?"

"She used to sing to me."

"But do you see what she did to you? Her and your father."

"What did they do to me?"

"They made you stronger because you understand fear."

I nod my head.

"What's this sign on your back?"

"It's a bull. Can you see its horns?"

I nod.

"And what's this sign on my wrist?"

"What does it look like to you?"

"It looks like a man sheep."

"You mean a ram."

"What does it look like to you?"

"It doesn't matter."

"Today is my birthday," I tell him.

"Liar. Today isn't your birthday and you know it. Do you see what your parents did to you?"

"No, Gerald."

"They taught you how to survive. I had to kill them so that you would learn never to spill another's blood. Blood frightens you, doesn't it?"

I look at him and think of saying yes but I don't.

"It isn't supposed to be on the outside," I tell him.

He laughs and drinks from the glass, all of it.

"Do you understand what Richard did to you?"

"No, Gerald. I'm stronger."

"He made you understand everything. You had to understand what hunger is, what thirst is."

"But I know that already."

"Let me finish," he raises his voice. The candle crackles.

"You had to understand everything so that you could live. People are trying to kill you."

"Who, Gerald, who?"

"Everyone. Gangsters, the mafia. Everyone. You had to understand that. You had to understand pain."

"But I hate pain." He sees my fear.

"You had to understand that. You had to understand what it means to be a woman. That's why they did that to you. I know that you understand what it means to be a woman already. You bleed through the anus when you shit, don't you?"

"I've always been like that."

"Your mother did that to you. She loved you too much. So much that you wanted to understand everything about being a woman. Do you know how evil that is?"

"No, Gerald."

"You say you're thirteen but your piel looks like you're five."

"I know that."

"Your father did that to you. That's why he was going to kill you. You didn't want to grow up so that you would always be with your mother. Do you see that?"

"No, Gerald."

"You must go back to Sea Point."

"And do what?"

"Let me finish," he raises his voice and the shack seems to shake a little. "You must go back to where you sleep. I've been watching you. I know where you stay. You must go back there and take a shit. And then you must never go back there."

"There is a woman I know there, she . . ."

"Forget about her. She's the one who sold you. All that money you made. She sold it to others so that they could make money out of you. The mother of evil. She's the devil herself. All that food she's been giving you. That's why you lose things. People have been stealing from you all your life. Your father knew this but still he beat you when you came home and said you lost things."

"I remember."

"He was cruel, your father. He made you wash in his dirty water. Do you know what that does to you?"

"No, Gerald."

"That's why you have blue eyes and love water. You're always thirsty because he did the same to your mother, before you were born. When you were in your mother's stomach you taught yourself how to swim, to love water because already in your mother's stomach you knew that dirty water is bad. Your father wanted to destroy you. The same way he killed his brother. He hated his brother enough to watch him being killed and he never did anything. He just watched and did nothing. He never cried. He should have cried. You know what happened? That water in his eyes turned to poison. That's why your father was evil. He made your mother wash in his dirty water. Do you know how evil that is?"

"No, Gerald."

"It is worse than killing someone. It is like pissing in milk and making someone drink it."

I pour myself some water and drink.

"Good," he says, "water has always saved you. But now you must stop washing in the sea. Do you understand?"

I look at him and say nothing.

He goes to the corner of the room and brings back two plastic dishes: a red one and an orange one. He closes the door and pours water from a clear plastic drum into both dishes. He gives me a little rag, the same one I used at the house Richard took me to. He also gives me Lifebuoy soap. I stand with one leg in the orange dish and wash. We both wash. I dry myself with the rag. He uses a towel. Afterwards I get dressed in my new clothes. He puts on his bright orange T-shirt and white jeans.

"Do you know what that is?" he says pointing to my T-shirt.
"A lion."

"No, that is a king, a predator."

"Like you?" I ask.

He smiles but his face doesn't light up. Instead I see all the creases and wrinkles it has gathered over the years. He has too many secrets.

"I'm tough. No one can destroy me except fire. That's why they had to burn Staggie to kill him. That was the only thing that could kill him. If they hadn't burned him the bullets would not have killed him," he says looking into my eyes. "Are you hungry?"

"No."

"Good. You must go now, the candlelight is going out." He puts out the candle by wetting his fingers and pressing them against the flame. White smoke rises. He breathes it in and opens the door.

"Come back tomorrow," he tells me.

12

I take my crutch outside and walk to Sea Point. I think about nothing but Joyce. I ring her doorbell when I get to the door. She opens it and starts shouting at me.

"Where've you been, wena? My food has been rotting out there. No one touched it." She pulls me by the wrist and lets me in.

"Sit," she tells me when I get into her small kitchen.

"Joyce, I need my money. I'm in trouble," I tell her.

"Hey, don't call me that," she says and slaps me across the face. "I'm old enough to be your grandmother." I look at her with surprise.

"Auntie, please, can you call the bank? I need my money."

"Your money? After all I did for you? You can't get that money. The bank won't give it to you," she says with cold eyes.

"You mean you won't give it to me."

She slaps me across the face again. Hard. My nose starts bleeding. I let the blood drip.

"Now see what you made me do," she says gently and runs to the toilet. She comes back with some toilet paper.

"Where's the blood?" she says finding my nose dry.

"I ate it."

"You're an evil child," she tells me and points her finger at me.

"I need my money," I tell her.

"What do you need it for? I give you food, don't I?"

"But I need it. I'm in trouble."

"Ja, you're in trouble because you're a naughty boy. See what you did to your leg. You're in trouble with the bank. You haven't been paying your money."

"What do you mean? I need the money," I tell her.

"Get out," she says, "you have caused me nothing but trouble. The bank is very angry with you."

"Fuck off," I tell her and she throws me out. She keeps my crutch.

"You will rot in your own piss," she tells me.

"Give me back my crutch!"

She slams the door in my face. Without thinking I open my pants and piss. I hear the seagulls. They screech. After pissing I spit into my piss and go.

My heart races with confusion and anger. What's wrong with this grown-up? Is she mad? I use the banister to get down the stairs. Outside many seagulls fly above me. They follow me as I struggle to walk. They scream and cry. I get onto the beach road and go towards Broken Bath beach. When I pass La Perla, the place where Joyce works, I spit. The seagulls dive near me in a mad frenzy and follow me as I limp to the beach.

The sun is still up and there are a few people on the beach. No, I say. No. I'm going to take a shit in their toilet. The seagulls gather near a large rock and wait. I spit where I used to sleep and tear up the clear plastic I used to sleep on. I leave it there and head towards the fountain.

Everybody I pass seems to be watching me. I drag my cast along. "Men" it says outside a door near the fountain. I spit first and go inside. I go into the first little room. There is piss on the seat. I wipe it clean and sit. I shit and think of Joyce. I spit in front of me. She was trying to kill me, I say to myself. All the money she stole from me is going to burn her. She will die, I tell myself. Joyce will die. An image comes to mind. I see a white man with black hair. I think hard about that image as I shit some more on top of the toilet paper. I know him, I say. He works at that place where they sell rude videos near that train. He has a pale face. I see an image of him doing it with Joyce. I spit as I shit. When I'm done I wipe myself again with lots of toilet paper. Joyce can have that. She earned it, I say to myself and flush. I watch the toilet swallow the mess. I wash my hands vigorously at the basin and avoid the mirror.

Outside I bump into Bafana. I'm pleased to see him.

"Where've you been, son?"

"What happened to your leg?"

"Nothing. A small thing really."

"I've got some zol. I was about to smoke it. Do you want some?"

My face lights up.

"Bafana, you must look after yourself. You see how I'm dressed? I don't live here anymore."

"I like your pants." He touches them. They sparkle in the light. "And that T-shirt? Who gave it to you?"

"Vincent."

"Oh, Vincent. I saw him today. He says he's going back home."

"Really?" I say. We walk to the moffie beach. They have a little place at the sea for them. It's like a big balcony. A black man watches as we sit there and roll a big zol.

"You can light it," Bafana says.

Bafana likes me because I look after him.

"So where are you going to stay now?" he says as I take the first drag. I close my eyes and let the smoke fill my lungs. I hear the seagulls nearby. They are going home to sleep.

"Are you hungry?" I ask him and pass the zol.

"No, finish. Leave some for me."

He's hungry.

"Look, you can't come where I'm going," I say. I can see that question in his eyes.

"You work for them now, don't you?"

"Who?"

"The gangsters."

I keep smoking. My shoulders drop. The calm settles over me and moves down my back all the way to my feet.

"I miss this," I tell him and watch the water rising and crashing in on itself.

Bafana looks thin. He looks thinner than when I last saw him.

"But you can find me in town where I park cars."

He smiles. He knows it means food. I give him the zol. He smokes it like he's holding a bottleneck. It burns quickly and is soon finished.

We sit there and listen to the waves. It feels like flying. I stretch out my arms and stand up to stretch out my back.

"They said Gerald fucked you up," he says.

I look at him and walk over to the water's edge. If only it was that simple, that easy, Bafana, I say to myself and spit into the water. I stand there and the wind blows. The sun is getting closer to the water. Boats go by. I wonder if they can see me. I wonder how far it is from here to them. They look small in the distance like toy boats. The black man walks beside me and also looks out over the water. He looks at me and grins. There is something familiar about his grin, something naughty about it. He looks like a bad man, the kind who would steal an old woman's bag.

I turn back. Bafana has left. I leave the beach and find a park bench to sit on.

13

My mind races with a million things. From where I'm sitting I can see everything. I can hear everything. All of it, the music, the patting of feet as people run, the dogs barking, cars rushing. I can hear it all, even my own heartbeat in my ear. And it all makes sense. Not good sense or bad sense, just sense. I scratch my balls and think about all the money Joyce stole from me. She's a bitch, a fucking cunt. It was a lot of money.

The moffies walk by. One of them looks at me but I pay no attention to him. I just look out at the sea. Another sits beside me and opens his legs. A big banana is between his legs.

"I like your pants," he says and brushes his shoulder against mine.

"You're full of kak," I hear myself saying.

He closes his legs but still sits beside me.

"What do you want?"

"You can sleep over if you want. You look clean."

I think about it and say nothing.

"Okay, I'll cook for you."

"Does your wife know you do this?"

"No. She's away on holiday," he says, looking a little nervous.

"Well, take off your ring. I don't want to see it," I almost shout at him.

"Done," he says and pulls it off.

"Why do you wear it?"

"Because I'm married."

"No. I mean . . ."

"Oh, I don't know. Habit, I guess. Also I don't want to lose it."

You've lost your mind, I say to myself.

"You have kids?"

"Look, I don't want to talk about my family. Are you coming or not?"

I look at him concealing his big banana and smile.

"I'm just waiting for the sun to go down."

We sit on the bench and say nothing as the sun gently touches the water. I always imagine that steam will go into the air when this happens but it never does. The sun just goes quietly into the water and disappears. The clouds become red with fire. On the other side of the sky I can see the colour of bruises.

"We better go," he says, "it's getting late."

You mean you're worried that someone might see you, I say to myself.

"I'll do it for fifty," I say as I get up.

"A bed, food and fifty. You drive a hard bargain," he says.

"Have you ever slept out here?" I say and look into his eyes.

He says nothing and walks in front. White people are full of kak, I say to myself.

We walk slowly as I don't have my crutch. Joyce, that bitch, I think.

"What happened to your leg?"

"I fell and broke it."

"What, your leg?"

"No, this part here," I say and point to my ankle.

"Is it sore?"

"Not really. I'll have it off in a couple of weeks. This thing, I mean."

"I know."

We go to his car first. He takes out two boxes and a plastic bag, the type dustbin people use. He gives me the plastic bag to hold. We go to a nice block of flats near Sunset Beach. It's the best block I've ever been to. Outside there's a guard.

"Hi, Alfred," he greets him as he lets me inside. When he's not looking Alfred gives me the evil eye. I stick out my tongue between my gap and cross my eyes.

"You better park your car in the garage, Mr Lebowitz, we've had some burglaries outside the building," he says in a deep grown-up voice.

"Fine, Alfred," he says as we get into the lift. We go up many floors, almost reaching the top floor. As we get out I look out of a row of large windows and see the sea.

"You live here?" I say.

He smiles and brushes my bum. We go into his flat. Almost everything is white. Strangely, I feel calm. He takes the plastic bag and offers me a seat. His manners are sickening. They are perfect and make you feel a little strange, like you're a dog with fleas. And he has to be careful around you. I ignore his manners and make myself comfortable. I sit on a white leather sofa. It's so soft I could fall asleep on it. He does something in the other room. I can hear cupboards opening and closing. I get bored and my eyes stray to the big TV. I'm shocked to see myself on the screen. I move closer and the image of myself moves closer as I move closer to the screen. I sit back and the image also sits back. For a while I just stare at myself stupidly. White people are evil, I say, and turn off the TV. I sit there and wait for him but I can't stop wondering about that TV. Where are the cameras? I wonder and look around the room. I can't see any cameras, only a neat room with lots of beautiful things. This guy is sick. He's going to film the whole thing.

"I thought we'd take a shower first," he says when he comes in.

"You mean you're horny?"

"Are you always this direct?"

"Do you want to fuck me?"

"Good God," he says and walks over to the piano where there are pictures of his family. He turns them all over as if they will see and hear everything.

"Look, if you're going to be like that you can get out now. I've tried being nice to you."

"Sorry," I say and grind my teeth.

"Just don't do it again."

"Look, that's how it is. They all speak to me like that."

"Well, I'm not them."

"Don't worry, I won't ask you your name."

"Good."

"Just relax, okay. I also want to have some fun," I lie and put on a smile.

"Well, I'm tense now," he says and goes to the other room.

"Can I put on the TV?" I ask.

"It's broken," he says and returns with a glass of wine.

"Is it all right if I take off my T-shirt? It's a little hot."

"Ja, sure, but I can put on the air-conditioning."

"Don't worry. I'll be fine," I say and take off my T-shirt.

"You've got the most incredible blue eyes for a . . ."

"Darkie," I smile.

"Yes," he says awkwardly. "Are they real?"

That is the strangest question I've ever heard.

"What do you mean?" I ask and sit closer to him.

"I mean, are they contact lenses?"

"What?"

"Never mind. I guess they're real."

He puts down his glass on the table. I put my hand on his

crotch and rub it. He opens his pants and his dick pops out. I stroke it gently.

"You like that, don't you?" I say while I rub it.

I know how to please a man. I know these bastards. I've done this a thousand times. They all like it if you play with the part between their balls and asshole. And you must not pull too hard on the dick. It's better if you play with the dick as close as possible to the tummy, otherwise they say it's sore or it starts flopping. And the older they get the more it doesn't stand up against their tummy. One guy's dick was still down but it was hard. And he wasn't that old. I think he had a problem with his piel. Poor bastard. Imagine having a broken piel.

Another thing is I never ask them how that feels. They hate that question. I think it reminds them of their boyfriends or their wives or whoever it is they are cheating on. The other thing is if you ask you get strange requests. I don't want to think about some of the things I've had to do to these bastards. No thank you.

"Let's go to the bathroom."

"Wait. I have a problem with my leg. I can't shower."

"Then you'll bath and I'll shower."

We go to the bathroom. It has white tiles on the floor that show off your reflection. And there is a large mirror on one wall. You can see your whole body when you get naked. And there are two toilet seats but one of them has little taps. It looks broken.

"I've never seen myself like this before," I say looking at the mirror.

"You mean naked?"

"No. I've seen myself naked before, just not on a mirror this big and with all this light."

"Oh," he says and runs a bath for me. I feel stupid for saying that.

"Are you hungry?"

"Not really," I lie and look at the white bath.

The taps are made of gold. Can you believe it, Blue? Gold. The fucking taps are made of gold. This guy must be loaded with baksheesh.

"Not too much," I say.

He closes the taps and gives me some soap and a towel. I get into the bath and hang my knee over the edge.

"Clever boy," he says and gets into the shower.

Fuck, I'm glad I washed at Gerald's. Imagine if he had to see my brown dirt.

We wash quickly and I clean out the bath with a sponge afterwards.

He gets out of the shower, his banana dick bouncing everywhere. He reaches out and strokes my face. I shake his dick and say "Pleased to meet you" like white people do. He laughs a little and takes my hand.

We go to his room. There is a large window and a bed far

away from the window. Sit here, he says, and goes to the window to close the curtains. I bounce a little on his big bed. It's nice and hard.

"Is this your room?"

"No, it's the guest room," he says and puts on the light.

He spreads me on the wide bed and starts sucking my dick. That's never happened before. I start giggling.

"Sorry, I've never had this," I say.

He ignores me and carries on. After a while the pleasure turns into sadness.

"I'll do it to you," I say.

He turns over and lies on his back. I take his banana dick in my hand and start stroking it. He lets out a long sigh. I play with his balls and the part underneath his balls. When I put my mouth on his head he moans a little and closes his eyes. I don't think about anything else. I just suck and play with my tongue on his banana dick. He starts breathing funny like he's going to pass out. Then he grabs my wrist and a fountain of sperm pours out of his banana dick and lands on his chest. It's over when that happens.

They all lie back and don't want to be touched. All that I can hope for now is that he will keep his other end of the bargain.

"Just give me some time," he says.

"You mean you still want to go?"

"Who's paying here?"

"I was only asking," I say and play with his balls.

After a while his banana dick rises again.

"Lie back," he says, "I want to come all over you. Do you mind?"

"No. Just don't squirt on my face."

He starts playing with himself while he stands over me. They all seem to enjoy this. I guess it feels like pissing to them.

After a while, a long while actually, he comes all over my chest. "Thank you," he says, "I've been dying to do that all day."

* * *

"It's a little hot, isn't it?" he says and puts on the air-conditioning.

I go to the toilet to get my clothes.

"Don't bother with them," he says.

We walk around the house naked. I have the feeling people are watching me, or rather that a camera is following me. He walks around in his slippers. I follow him to the kitchen. He opens a large silver door and a cold breeze comes out. The shelves are stacked with food.

"What do you fancy? We can either have turkey on our sandwich or cheese."

"Turkey and cheese," I say.

He takes them both out and a cabbage. I watch him prepare the food. He's good with his hands.

"So what do you do?" I ask him. "If you don't mind."

"I'm an investment banker."

"But what do you do?"

"I work with lots of money."

"It must be a hard job," I say.

"It is."

"So you work here in Cape Town?"

"That's right."

Investment banker. He's probably the bastard who took my money, I say, thinking of Joyce.

"So is it hard for anyone to open a banking spot at your place?"

"You mean opening an account. I'm afraid I don't do that sort of work."

"Oh. So you're like the boss."

"Something like that. I have a lot of people working for me. But I know what you're talking about."

We sit at the table. He pours me some orange juice in a tall glass.

"This is strange," I tell him.

"What?"

"Walking and eating naked like this."

"You don't like it?"

"No, it just feels strange. But a good strange."

He chews with his mouth closed. As always I eat quickly.

"Had enough?" he asks, after I have finished four slices of bread.

"Yes."

I wanted to say thank you but it just wouldn't come out. We go to the other room with the big television. He puts on some music.

"You know what this is?"

"No, but I've heard it before."

"Classical music. Carl Orff, *Carmina Burana*. He's like your . . . rap artists or whatever you listen to."

He sits on a chair for one and grabs some cigarettes from the table beside him.

"Can I have one?" I ask as he lights one.

He takes one out but he doesn't pull it all the way out of the pack. He offers me the one pointing at me. His manners are maddening. I can see him. He thinks about everything all the time.

We smoke in silence and listen to the music. The songs are long. But I like the music. It does something to your insides. It lets you relax.

"But this music is violent," I say after a while.

"It is, isn't it? *Carmina Burana* is not for the faint-hearted. Listen to this part."

The strings reach fever pitch and people sing around beating drums.

"What is that instrument?"

"Violin."

"You like music, don't you?"

"Ssssh," he says, "listen."

I listen with him for about thirty minutes and fall asleep. He wakes me. He's already dressed.

"I just need to park the car in the garage downstairs. Don't get up to any mischief. Oh, and you can't leave the building without me. So just behave. I'll be back in a while," he says and leaves.

As soon as he leaves I put on the TV again. This time the TV shows the room we were doing it in. I go in there and look for the cameras but I can't find them. It starts feeling creepy walking around the house naked. Is this guy a pervert or something? I say as I put on my clothes. I walk around the rooms but only in the ones where the doors are open. In two of them the doors are locked. So this is how people who work in banks live. They are always being watched. I wouldn't want all his money if it meant I had to live like that. To always have people watching you is a curse. I turn off the TV.

I sit on the couch. I start to feel a little sad. No, I tell myself. I must be strong. I am strong. I get up and go to the kitchen. I drink from the tap, my mouth around its mouth. I drink lots till my stomach says enough. I feel better, I tell myself and go back to the couch. Why do you feel sad? I ask myself. Because my mother didn't love me. Gerald is cruel. That is the ugliest thing anyone has ever said to me. It is worse than having a bus crush you. I think of my mother and feel confused. No. She loved me, I tell myself. And I loved her, no matter what Gerald says. He's just like Allen. He wants to control me. I look around and realise that there are no stupid pigeons watching me, only hidden cameras. You're never completely on your own, I say. Only when you are born and when you die. Nobody cares when you die. They just want to know what you will leave them. I remember my father saying that about my grandfather after he died. I hope he left me that watch, he kept saying. He never did get it. The relatives came before we did and cleaned out my grandfather. I don't want to think about my family. But you have to, a little voice says inside me.

What's there to think about? My mother died. My father died. I hiked to Cape Town with Mandla, Vincent. And now I'm here. There's nothing much to say. There's nothing much to think about. I can't write. I can't phone my relatives. They don't care about me anyway. And I don't miss them. I don't miss them because they never gave me anything. And that's all right, at least they didn't give me bullshit like Cape Town grown-ups. I feel better when I say this. You see. Sea Point. I'm getting stronger.

* * *

He returns and finds me with my clothes on.

"I thought we'd have another go," he says.

I take off my clothes in the room. His banana dick bounces out of his pants again as he takes them off.

"Wait," he says and runs into the other room. He puts on the music, different music but still the same whining, stringy music.

"Vivaldi, *Four Seasons*. I've always wanted to do this."

He lies on top of me and just grinds his hips against mine.

"Why aren't you getting an erection?" he says.

I think of Toni Braxton and my dick rises.

"That's better," he says and carries on rubbing himself against me. "This time I want you to come with me."

"Ready when you are."

"Really? Just like that."

"It's true."

"Okay, wait. I'll tell you."

He doesn't tell me. His eyes just start rolling into their whites and he grunts to the music.

"Oh heaven," he says as the music rises. "Are you coming too?"

"Yes," I say and nearly laugh at the funny look on his face.

Then he falls flat on me and sighs.

"That was great. You killed me. I'm completely annihilated."

"It doesn't take much," I say.

"You and the music," he says and gets up to wipe himself. He throws the towel at me. Strange, he usually hands me things.

We both put on our clothes and go to the music room. He sits on the chair and smokes alone.

"You like this music, don't you?"

He says nothing. He looks sad, a little angry or hurt. I can't tell. Grown-ups are hard to figure out.

"It's Winter," he says.

"What?"

"The music. It's called *Four Seasons* and now it's Winter."

I listen.

"Listen carefully. Can you see the trees without leaves?"

Trees. I know trees. I listen to the music. It is too much. I go into the other room and sit on the couch. This guy is trying to open me up. He thinks he's clever. Of course he's clever, he owns a bank. Him and Joyce are all from the same team. Don't forget that, I remind myself.

"I feel tired," I say when he comes back.

"I was going to play you this one song by Mussorgsky."

"I'm really tired," I say and put on puppy eyes.

"Okay, come," he says.

We go back to the room. He opens the bed.

"Will this pillow be enough? I can get you another one if you want."

"No, it's fine. Actually I like sleeping without one."

The street, I can hear him thinking, but his maddening manners prevent him from saying it.

"Where are you going to sleep?"

"I don't know. I might sleep in here. I don't know. Good-night." He switches off the light and leaves the door open.

* * *

I get into bed but sleep doesn't come easily. I stare at the ceiling and try not to think much. Too much thinking is bad for you. Look at all the grown-ups I know. They're all fucked in the head. They should be smoking zol. And that poor bastard in there, he doesn't know whether to leave or to come. At least I have new pants and a T-shirt. But I'll need a new jacket for the days when it gets cold. I know. I'll buy a jacket from that place in Long Street. I'm sure I can get something there. But I must be careful. I mustn't buy like a moegoe. I must buy a sensible jacket. Vincent said I must be the blackest person he knows. I still don't understand what he means by that. He said I must buy from makwerekwere. I can if I want to now; I don't have to think about Allen. And I don't think Gerald will mind. In fact I think Gerald wants me to do things for myself. I'm not going to ask him. I'm just going to buy it. That's right. No thank you, Gerald. I'm just going to buy it.

Now if only I could sleep. My neck hurts. I must sleep now. Tomorrow I'm going to get a new jacket. That's something to look forward to. And I don't have to look at Allen anymore or Joyce, that bitch. I hope she gets boils all over her pussy and that stupid white man who does ugly things in the dark with her. I hope his piel rots. They're both evil. But I'll miss Sea Point. I'll still come back when I can. I just won't go anywhere near them. I'll just stay on the beach road. And I'll buy a towel and maybe one day I can take a dip in that pool and buy myself ice cream like I always say I will. It's all going to be fine. I can take their bullshit. All of them. Even Gerald.

But I hope Vincent doesn't go. Why did Bafana say that? Was he also fucking with me? No, Bafana likes me. He wouldn't say that unless it was true. Vincent can't go. He's my connection. The only one I have in Cape Town. Without him I'll have no one. And everyone has a connection, even if it's just one person in the whole word. No, he can't go. I'll talk to him tomorrow. I think of Vincent as my eyes. He's older than me. He's seen more, done more. I don't think anything scares him any more. Everything seems to make sense to him. Vincent, he's grown-up but not like the others. He doesn't bullshit. He just says it like it is. And sometimes it isn't pretty. But that doesn't worry him. He just stays Vincent, Mandla; the guy I grew up with in Mshenguville. He's all right, Vincent. He always looks out for me. All the things he tells me, they help me. They help me become like him, a man, a grown-up.

He changes the music. The saddest music I ever heard comes out. But it's a gentle sadness that doesn't take you all at once. It just goes by you but you feel it. It's a soft sadness. I look at the light coming through the room and wonder what he's doing. But I'm too tired to get up. I just listen to the music while I beg sleep to come.

I can hear the piano. The softest notes seem to fly. Rising and falling like a seagull flying. This guy is fucked, I say to myself. To listen to music like this you must be fucked. And he probably listens to it while his wife is there but she doesn't know what's going on in his head. That's fucked, I say, and listen to the notes rapidly playing before they disappear into quiet, slow notes. The music always ends gently. When the song ends I close my eyes and grab all the sleep I can get in this warm room.

14

He wakes me up early before sunrise and tells me to put on my clothes. There is something different about him. He avoids my eyes as he goes in and out of the room to check if I'm getting dressed. He is already dressed in a suit. For some reason I think of a tree when I see him. The suit makes him look taller. It makes him look like one of those trees that grow straight and tall and have needles. And they are always green.

He gives me a hundred bucks and lets me out of his flat. Alfred watches me like a cat. He watches both of us but makes as if he's reading his newspaper. "Morning, Mr Lebowitz," he says. He looks at him and gives him a short "Hi, Alfred." I bet Alfred sees this all the time when Mrs Lebowitz is away on holiday with the kids. But he says nothing. He works for them. He has to listen to their shit.

I hold the money in my pocket and go. I think of my crutch when I walk. I wonder what that stupid bitch is going to do with it. I stay on the beach road and walk towards Green Point. It's a long walk because I have to be careful with the other leg. I see Allen on the other side of the road. He's wearing his RayBans. They are so dark you can never tell who he's look-ing at when he wears them. But I know he can see me. I know he can see my pants shining in the light. He's a prick, I say to myself as I walk. A girl stands on the road near him. A different white girl with long, blonde hair. He only works with white girls. I guess because they are easier to control. Even though they have big mouths one klap usually shuts them up if they're not on crack. That other bitch who got beaten up when I was there was stupid. She was hooked on crack and she had a big mouth like the coloured girls. They're full of shit, coloured girls. They've got dirty mouths and they never wait. When they see a man walk by, any man, they try to tempt him with their pussy. "Hey, baby, do you want some?" and if the man doesn't want to pay two hundred bucks for a full house and a happy ending they are the first to swear at him. "Jou ma se poes, man!" Now the black girls are different. There's always something angry and quiet in their eyes. Black girls talk with their eyes. They look at you and you either know what you want or you just keep walking. I always look at the ground when I pass them. I know their strength and fear it. Some of them look like they could crush a man with their powerful thighs. They look like they can make any bastard come.

I pass Green Point and go towards town. Even though it's hot I still think of buying a jacket. I go near Subway and don't find Vincent there. I find him at his usual hang-out place where he sleeps all night. He sits near the pavement with a torn bag.

"I've been waiting for you, bra."

"Don't tell me it's true."

"I have to go sometime," he says.

"Why? What are you running away from?" I say as I carefully sit next to him.

"From you," he jokes.

"This is serious. You're leaving me. You're my only connection in Cape Town."

"You'll be all right."

"Can I come with you?"

"You don't have enough money. I've been saving up. I'm going by train."

"But you can't leave. They'll kill me if you leave."

"No one's going to kill you. You're with Gerald, remember?"

I don't know what to say and feel sad.

"Just remember, if you're ever in trouble always go towards the light. Okay?"

"But you're leaving."

"Blue, Azure, listen to me, okay? If you're ever in trouble, always go towards the light."

"Vincent isn't your real name, is it?" I say changing the subject.

"No, they gave it to me."

"Who?"

"Cape Town. The people. You know who I'm talking about."

"I don't like Blue."

"But it's yours now. You're wearing the pants."

"What if I run away?"

"Don't be stupid."

"They stole my money."

"How much?"

"I don't know but a lot."

"Don't worry, it's going to burn them."

"That's what I said."

He gets up to go.

"What about my tackies?"

"Gerald has them, he'll give them to you when he's ready. You must look after yourself, bra. Do you understand that? No one's going to help you in Cape Town. You must do everything yourself."

"You mean, I mustn't trust anyone with my money?"

"You know what I mean. Money is complicated. It's like people. It keeps changing. Sometimes it's your friend, sometimes it's your enemy. Don't trust money too much. It always lets you down in the end. Look at me. When I came to Cape Town I had a suitcase. Look at me now," he says and I look at his torn bag.

"There's nothing much in here," he says, "but it's my stuff. You check what money is?"

I walk with him to the station. He doesn't look sad that he's going. He looks strong, like wherever he ends up he'll be able to breathe.

"So where are you going? Are you going back to Joburg?"

"Fuck no. To what? I haven't seen my family in three years. No, I'm going to PE."

"Oh," I say. He'll miss Cape Town.

"But I've heard East London is better."

We pass the ticket office.

"This is where I get on," he says.

He looks at the old train posing in one corner of the station.

"Look, I used to copy from you in school; now you copy everything I said and you'll be fine," he says and hugs me.

He's the only person who ever hugs me.

"You're my big brother," I say, "I never had a big brother."

"Just look out for yourself and remember if you're ever in trouble . . ."

"Always go towards the light," I say.

He smiles.

"I'll see you around," he says and leaves.

I don't wait for him to get on the train, I start going. I walk around the station and feel lost. With Vincent I'm never lost. I always know where I'm going because I'm walking with him. No, don't say it, I tell myself, and resist saying I'm going to miss him. You're getting stronger, I tell myself. Very strong. I look at the lion showing its teeth on my T-shirt and think of

Gerald. T-rex wants me to be strong. He's watching, listening. I see pigeons outside. They sit on the lawn and don't look so stupid.

I go to Long Street. I go to the shop where the woman sold me veldskoene. But she isn't there. Another younger one is there. She looks like she smokes zol because she greets me when I come through the door.

"Funky eyes," she says. I smile at her whiteness.

In the back I go through a rack. It doesn't take long before I find a jacket that fits me. A black bomber jacket. And the price is right. It says seventy-five. But it worries me because it's orange on the inside and Gerald said I mustn't wear that colour. But I feel a little dangerous as Vincent has left and decide to buy it.

"Funky jacket," she smiles again as I pay. I can smell zol under her breath and smile. I wish more people like her gave it to her kind.

I wink at her as I go.

"That's right, man. Thanks is way overrated," she winks back. I don't understand what she said but it felt right to wink at her.

I wear my bomber jacket even though it's hot outside. It shines in the light. Then I buy myself a chip roll and juice and go to the Gardens to eat. I have twenty bucks left. What am I going to do with it? Vincent always said I mustn't flash around notes. Fine, I can break it into two fives and a ten. But now what am I going to do with fifteen bucks? I don't want to spend it. And I know Gerald will give me my tackies, at least I hope so. So there's no point saving it for shoes. Besides, where can I put it? That stupid bitch took all my money.

I lie on the grass and think about what I can do with my money. An answer doesn't come at once so I take a nap. I sleep deeply and dream of being on a boat at sea. But then I wake up suddenly, my heart beating very fast. I breathe in deeply and sigh when I realise that I'm lying under a tree. I dreamt I was at sea and that I had fallen out of a boat but no one had seen me. The boat just kept going and I was beginning to drown. And it was at night too. It was a scary dream. To be alone in the sea, at night and without a soul or land nearby, what could be worse? I decide to hide my money. But there's no place safe enough in town. I think about where I can hide my money. The sleeping mountain is above. I look at it for a long time and then an answer comes to me. On the mountain, I can hide my money on the mountain, I say. It's safe enough. But I can't get there. My leg is still in a cast. I get frustrated and decide to spend all the money. I buy ice cream twice and three pies and I still have something left over to buy zol.

I go to the bridge to Liesel.

"Two stops," I say to her and hand her the money over her little fence.

She takes it and says nothing. There's something different about her. We've lost that thing we had between us. We used to talk. We used to talk about kwaito and other things we liked. But now she won't talk to me. And I know what it is. It's because I stay here now. And she thinks I've become one of them.

She comes back with the two stops and goes back to whatever she was doing. I sit near Ma Zakes and tear some paper from the Yellow Pages. I roll a long zol. One of the old bergies comes to me. "Skyf?" he asks and nearly falls over. I ignore him and smoke.

"Hey! Tsek, jou naai," I hear Gerald say.

He walks over to me like he's going to beat me up. I cover my head. He grabs me by the scruff and shouts at me to stand up. I get up but still cover my head.

"Why did you buy that jacket?" he says.

"Because I can keep warm," I say.

"What did I say to you?"

"You said I mustn't wear your colour but it's on the inside," I beg.

He lets go of me and goes to the boot of his car. He takes out a saw and comes walking towards me like a madman. Oh fuck, I say. He's going to chop me up into small pieces. He grabs my bad leg and starts sawing at the case.

"So you want to be a man?" he says while he saws.

I say nothing. I just pray that he doesn't saw off my leg. White dust goes everywhere.

"You want to be a man? Answer me, jou naai."

"No, Gerald."

"Fuck you. I know you want to be a man. You want to see what I'm really about? Huh? I'll show you. Jou fokken naai. Jy's vol kak nè? Poes."

He cuts me a little bit but I don't wince. He sees the blood.

"This is what you want, isn't it?"

"No, Gerald. No," I plead.

"Tsek, jou naai." He continues sawing. "I told you not to wear that colour, didn't I? Didn't I? Answer me, jou naai, or I'll cut you up with this."

I nod my head. When the case is nearly off he rips it off with his powerful arms and throws it at the toilet.

"Now voetsek, jou poes!" He kicks me. I run away till I get to the main road. My head is spinning with confusion. Surprisingly my ankle doesn't hurt. I take off my shoe and hold it. I walk fast and don't think about where I'm going. I just walk. I go into town and walk into the Gardens. I throw my shoe into a bin. My heart racing, I keep on walking, looking behind me to see if Gerald is there. Pigeons fly everywhere in the Gardens. I'm suspicious of them. A dog barks at me but its owner grabs it by the leash. A man looks at me strangely because I don't have shoes. I tell him to fuck off with my eyes. In everyone I pass I can see a little of myself. I carry a little of everyone I know in me.

15

I walk past the government buildings, past the ugly statue of the man on a horse. I head for the mountain panting like a beast. It is hot. I open my jacket. No, fuck him. Fuck Gerald, I say and take off my jacket. I turn it inside out and wear the orange colour on top.

Destroy, destroy, my feet burn as I walk on the hot tar road and pavement. Whenever I can I walk in the shade. But I keep the pace fast, no matter if there is sun or shade. I just keep walking. The road gets steeper as I get up. I pass a quiet neighbourhood where the only sound you'll hear is the sound of dogs barking behind closed gates. I walk past a cricket field where white schoolboys practise in the nets. I walk past them with furious energy. They don't say anything, just watch me go into the trees. I watch the ground as there are broken bottles everywhere. I slow down and walk carefully. Gerald is behind me. My T-shirt is wet with sweat and anger. Destroy them, I hear my feet say as sharp stones punish my feet. I walk and keep shaking out my ankle every once in a while. I'm strong, I tell myself. When I'm tired I sit on a rock in the shade and look above. The sun burns with fire. I stick out my tongue and pant like a dog. A mad, animal energy rushes through me. I'm going to destroy them, all of them. I tell myself. I take off my jacket and wrap it around my waist. I keep climbing, going further, higher.

I pass a little lake where white people are swimming. They lie in the shade and swim in the sun, their children walking around naked like little gods. They go everywhere. I stare at the sun and then I look at them. I only see circles of fire. I keep walking. I go up a stony path till I get to the bottom of the mountain where there are only trees and rocks. I sit on a rock and roll myself a zol, my last stop. I roll it slowly and think about all the people I'm going to destroy. My body tenses, my muscles flex. You're getting stronger, I tell myself as I light my zol. I take long, deep drags that fill my head with madness. The zol is clean. It gives me fire. When I look at the sun I can still see destruction. Total destruction.

My heart beats loudly. You're alive, it says. The air smells clean. I'm thirsty, I say as I get up to go. I walk up a large black rock. A little stream trickles down it. I lick the water off the rock and it tastes good. I don't drink much. I keep walking. My legs move quickly. My arms grab easily. I pass dead trees and trees that were burned. The black trunks make me wild with pleasure. I move quickly, like a rat, crawling over everything. I'm stronger, I keep saying, I'm going to destroy them. I come out at a path that takes me onto a road. When I look back I can see the city. The mountain stands high above it. It stands there like a giant that is about to move and crush everything in its way. I stare at the sun again and feel its wild energy. Feed me. Feed me, I plead with my eyes. My muscles get tighter. The veins running down my arms stand out. I begin the final stage. I go up the mountain.

I walk for a long time before I decide to take off my T-shirt. I also wrap it around my waist. I pass many people, mostly white people and the kind that sound like they come from overseas. They stare and look and point to this and that. Everything is new to them. I pass them in a flash, the rocks scraping at my tough, hard feet. But I don't bleed. I just keep climbing, higher and higher. I get excited when I think of this ball of fire growing bigger and destroying everything in its path. I feel the sun's heat on my back. I take in the heat with pleasure and sweat it out. I'm cleaning myself, I say. When I tire I sit in the shade and try to follow the sun. It also climbs higher and higher and starts going down the other side. I'll see you on the other side of the mountain, I say as I get up to climb. Faster, faster.

The madness is inside me. The sun burns hot. Lizards crawl in my path. I go up further, the rocks tearing at me. I come across a dog and its owner. He sees me glistening with sweat. I stand in the sun and look at him. My pants shine and my body is wet, also shining. I suck my teeth and he sees the madness in my eyes. He says nothing. The dog sniffs around me. I pass them. I get to a stream. The water is clear. I wash my face and hands first before I drink. I take in as much water as I can. But I don't drink too much. You must climb higher. Higher. I finish drinking and look at the sun. I stare at it with open eyes and feel energy going through me. It mingles with the zol in my head and gives me fire. I get to the part where there is only shade. My body cools down but I don't slow down. Fire! Fire! I must give them fire, I tell myself. Higher.

When I look back I can see the now-quiet city. It lies weak beneath me. I spit. I'm going to crush you, I tell myself and step up. I start to see the top. Birds with long wings fly there like guardians of the mountain. Animals with lots of hair that look like big cats come out to see me. They have small tails and are fat. I pass them and go up towards the light. The walls of the mountain get closer as I get near the top. I get up the steps that seem to lead to a door without the top part. The top part leads to the sky, to the sun, to fire! I move up into the light.

You reached the top, I tell myself as I look at grey-white rocks. I can hear people on my right. I go left. I climb a little further up and walk as if I know where I'm going. The sun is slowly going down on the other side. Faster, faster, it says. I move with it and keep walking. The top eventually levels out. I can see far. Ahead of me are more mountains and the sea. It just seems to go on forever. I pass more people but they say nothing to me and I have nothing to say to them. I'm done with grown-ups. They are full of shit. They want fire. I'll give them fire. I move towards some rocks in the distance. The mountain air makes my head dizzy with its cleanliness. I dodge the wet patches on the ground. I roll my pants up to my knees and keep going. My sweat drips. My waist is wet.

I get to the rocks and the sun seems to smile. I can hear insects, birds whispering. He is mad, they say. He is mad. I keep going. Eventually the ground becomes flat again. I can see the edge of the mountain. That is where I'm going. I'm going to the edge, I tell myself. Destroy them, I say as I get closer. I begin to see the city again. It moves closer. The only sound I can hear below is the big boats coming in. They hoot and look like toys from up here. Fire! Fire!

I go through tall grass and wonder what my feet are stepping on. But it is all wet and soft. I keep walking and opening the tall grass. Closer. I get to dead trees that have been cut down. The ones that look like Mr Lebowitz. The ones that grow straight and have needles. I will make fire with them, I say.

The sun has gone down the other side but it is still light. Must find a place to sleep, I tell myself. I jump over a stream and climb up a wall of rocks. Dead trees are scattered everywhere. I scramble up a rock till I get to a small cave. This is where I'll sleep, I laugh. I won. I'm going to destroy them. I walk into the cave and see ashes. Someone has put stones around the ashes. It is big enough for me and the fire. And it is a closed cave. The wind will stay outside. I bend down to get out and move closer towards the edge. There is a drop that leads to more rocks. I jump over it onto another large rock. From there I can see the city. It is windy up here. And a large bird floats by. *Kwaa!* It opens its sharp beak and circles before it goes. My heart slows and I start to feel cold. I take off my wet T-shirt and jacket.

I jump back to the other side and go through a tunnel. I come out in the sun. I lay my clothes on a rock and go below to get some wood. I feel happy and miss nothing. I don't feel hunger and I don't feel thirst. I just feel myself. I feel strong. I jump from one rock to another like a buck, a small buck. But I am careful. I shake out my ankle and think of Gerald. He thought he was going to destroy me. I'll give him fire. I'll give him destruction. I'll give them all destruction, I say and start gathering wood. I take the dead ones, the ones that look grey and white from too much drying in the sun. They will burn easily, I say, and leave the brown ones. It is hard work carrying them up and down and through the tunnel but I enjoy it. I work silently. For the first time I work like I know what I'm doing. I don't think too much. I choose wisely. That one will do. No, that one is still green. No, that one is heavy. That one is light. That one looks like a snake. That one looks like a leg. I pick the ones I like, the ones that look like something. I carry back arms, legs, bodies, birds, elephants, monsters with many arms and legs and other things. I even see one that looks like a head with a long neck. I pile them outside the cave.

I go to the stream. I take off my pants while it is still light and wash. I wash my face first and think about what I'm about to do. I wash and ache to swim. I splash lots of water. No one watches me. It is quiet all around. I sit on a large warm rock and dry. The sun has gone down. It knows what I'm about to do. It knows my secret. It is warm. I thought it would get cold. From below you always see a white cloud hanging over the mountain like a wet cloth and you think it must be cold up there. But there are few clouds in the sky. Tomorrow, I say, I will go there. I climb down the rocks and jump over the stream. I put on my pants and they are still clean. I get my jacket and T-shirt from the slab coming out the wall. I go into the tunnel. It is darker in here.

I must work quickly before it gets dark. I take small branches and pack them into a triangle in the middle of the circle of stones. Then I light the fire but it dies. I go outside and tear up longish strings of dried grass. I roll them up into a ball. And then I take dried needles from the Lebowitz tree. I put the needles and the dried grass between the gaps in the triangle. I light the dried grass and needles. They crackle and burn quickly. The branches also catch the fire. They start burning. I blow to encourage the fire. Feed me, it says. I go outside and come back with more branches. I feed the fire slowly, making sure that all the branches are on fire. And when the ends are not on fire, I push them into the flames. It burns slowly at first. I watch it, my eyes smiling with fire. When I see that the fire is burning properly I bring in the first victim. I bring in a branch that looks like an arm.

I place it carefully over the fire. It burns easily. It was begging for destruction. I watch the flames cover it. A quiet hissing sound fills the cave. The arm starts turning black. Its skin peels off. I watch the fire eating it. Underneath, the branches are orange hot. It is hell in here and I'm the devil, I say. Let's get T-rex. I go outside again and return with a branch that looks like a monster's head. I put it on top of the arm. There is some dried fluff around it. It is the first to burn. Ja, Gerald, I say as I look at the monster's head. Burn. You want fire, don't you? You want me to burn you, don't you? And then I think of something. I take off my T-shirt and look at my jacket. Then all of a sudden the fire gets too big and feels hot against my face. I get out of the cave and give it space.

Outside I can see smoke rising, drifting into the sky. And I can hear the stream running outside. It is quiet and dark. And the moon is out; all of it. I feel calm and fear nothing. I climb onto the roof of the cave. The rocks seem to glow in the moonlight and the orange of my jacket also seems to glow. The rocks look like strange creatures. They have horns and some of them look like people from afar.

16

I have never been on my own this long in Cape Town. It feels good. I don't feel rushed. I sit in a pothole in the rock that looks like it was shaped for sitting. The sun has become the moon. All the cats will be roaming the streets. The moon does that to them. They can't sleep and stay awake to bury their secrets outside. I don't like cats much. They don't really need people. There's something stubborn and alone about them. And in their eyes you can see that they are smart. They know things, like what to do when the moon is out.

I stand up to take a piss. The water glistens in the moonlight. I think of the seagulls and what they did for me that day on the roof.

I go back to the cave and find that the fire is almost out. It is dark in there. I get more dried grass and needles. I put them on the red embers and put small branches on top. They burn quickly. I add more branches. The fire picks up. Feed me. Feed me, it says begging me for total destruction. I bring in a monster with many arms and legs. I break off its limbs and throw them in the fire. They burn and the skin peels. When I throw in the rest of the monster the fire jumps a little and makes a hissing noise like it's watching me. I watch the flames play with all the colours of the rainbow. But I like orange best. I like the burning embers underneath. The more I watch the fire, the more I feel like dancing. I take off my jacket and put it in the corner. It will be my bed. Then I start slapping my thighs like a drum. My back straightens and I close my eyes. The smoke fills my head. The fire makes me sweat.

I close my eyes and see the night. I sway my neck, drums playing in my head. I slap my thighs. The fire burns. I start to travel through the night. I see a grey wolf running in the moonlight. With powerful paws it leaves its prints on the ground. I move with the speed of this wolf. It runs to the edge of a cliff and becomes a big bird that spreads itself across the sky. It holds a rat in its mouth. The bird flies to its nest and feeds its babies. They tear up the meat. I feel their hunger. I drift again till I see a monster in the darkness. It breathes fire but it is dark like the night. Its skin is made of darkness and stars like the night. When it moves you see stars moving in a string. It moves in the form of the number eight and breathes fire. Fire! It breathes fire, this beautiful monster, and fills the sky. I move with it and follow it. It goes higher and higher into the air. I follow it. I move further and further away from the ground. I move so far away from the earth that it becomes smaller and smaller till I can only see a ball. I keep following the monster that breathes fire. Every time I think I've lost it, it opens its mouth and out comes fire. We move past many balls and in the distance I start to see a murky soup. We get closer and the soup becomes stars. Millions and millions of stars that look like floating diamonds. We move through many colours and soups and stars. Then we start to see the sun. It is a large fireball with brilliant explosions.

I start to feel warm as I get closer to the sun. I watch the monster go into the fire. A big explosion happens. *Boomda!* I take in a deep breath and open my eyes. There is a man standing at the entrance of the cave. He startles me.

"Can I come in?" he says.

I wipe my face of sweat and call him in with my arm. I wonder how long he was standing there. He bends down to come in. The first thing I see in the light is his long brown hair. He is wearing sandals, shorts and a vest. He also carries a bag. He leaves it outside the cave, there isn't enough space inside. I watch him closely. He sits next to me and stretches his hands towards the fire like he's greeting it.

"I've been walking all day. The night caught up with me."

"Oh," I say and study him.

"My name is Oscar," he says and reaches out to shake my hand. He has a firm grip. "And yours?"

"Just call me Blue."

"Okay, Blue."

He has a funny way of speaking.

"You're not from around here, are you?"

"Who is in Cape Town?" he says and ties his hair back. He has powerful arms. I can see his arm muscles flexing and aching to do something.

"Nice fire."

"Nice place to sleep, don't you think?"

"Yes, but I don't think there's enough room for two."

"Ja," I say and look at him. You're making yourself welcome, I think, smiling.

He takes out a small pouch from his bag and some Rizla. I watch him closely. He rolls a joint.

"Cherry tobacco." He smiles as he lights it.

"Ah," I say stupidly, but it isn't like that. I'm just comfortable.

I go outside to get some more wood. I bring back a snake and hope for the best. I put it carefully in the fire. He takes small puffs and plays with the smoke, blowing out small circles and other interesting things to watch. He passes me the last half of his joint. A nice cherry smell fills the cave.

"You come here often?"

"No," I say. I wanted to say yes but decided against it.

"I stay on the other side in Hout Bay."

"You mean you walked from there?"

"Ja."

"It isn't that far," I say and he is not surprised to hear me say that.

"Then you must walk a lot."

"I do."

He looks at my feet but says nothing. He takes off his glasses and rubs his eyes and then he puts his glasses on again. He goes to his bag and takes out something. He brings back a silver thing and starts unwrapping it. He offers me four slices of bread. He eats the other four. He doesn't waste time. He crunches into his food. He probably smokes zol, I smile inside, and eat my food quickly. We just about finish at the same time.

"What was that thing?"

"Hummus and cheese."

"What?"

"Hummus," he says licking his fingers. "I make it myself."

"It's nice."

We go outside to have a drink in the stream.

"How did you find this place?" I ask him.

"I was lost. It was dark. I saw smoke in the distance. So I went towards it," he says and kneels down to drink. I put my face near the water and suck.

"And you?"

"First time here. I found it by luck."

"You tired?"

"Not really," he says and splashes his face. "It's nice and hot though."

"Pity there isn't a pool around here."

"Actually there's a nice reservoir on the other side."

"How far is it?"

"About two hours' walk there."

I think about it.

"Take me there."

"Are you crazy?"

"There's plenty of light."

He rubs his hair and thinks about it.

"How will we ever find this place when we get back?"

"I check."

"We can always go tomorrow."

He's inviting himself again, I say.

"Where did you say you were from?" I ask as we sit on a rock.

"Hout Bay. After Clifton and Camps Bay."

"Okay, now I see. So you must be rich."

"You never told me where you come from." He ignores my comment.

"I live under a bridge."

"Which one?"

"The one near Green Point."

"Oh, you mean the one that was under construction but was never completed."

"If it is, I never noticed."

"Ja, it's an incomplete bridge. I've heard weird stories from there."

"Like what?"

"Well, there's this guy who lives there, right, and he's supposed to control the entire rat population in Cape Town. It's kind of an urban legend."

"That's nothing. I know a guy who lives there and he can make anyone, take you right, he can change you into a pigeon or a rat."

"It's probably the same guy I'm talking about."

"I doubt it. He never leaves that place. When he does he's always in his car."

"What does he drive?"

"A white Ford Grenada."

"Lot of white cars in Cape Town. Ever noticed that?"

"No."

"Anyway, people are always talking shit. You never know anything really unless you're there," he says.

"I know what you mean. Ja, it's like have you ever tried to explain what it feels like to swim, to someone who's never been in water like that?"

"No."

"It's crazy. You can't. I tried to explain swimming to this one friend of mine called Liesel but she's being a bitch to me. And I couldn't."

"I get like that when I talk about the mountain."

"What do you do?"

"It doesn't matter. Nobody understands why I do this three times a week."

"How long have you been here?"

"Three months."

"Don't worry, it's normal. She's bad, Cape Town. She takes you in, in the beginning, but be careful. She'll destroy you if you're not watching."

"That's what my boyfriend says."

I'm a little surprised.

"I didn't think you were a moffie," I say.

"Whatever," he says.

"I work with them."

"What do you mean, you work with them?"

I pat my dick.

"Oh I see, that sort of thing. Well, I'm not into that."

"Good, 'cause I was about to tell you to fuck off," I joke.

He doesn't take it kindly but doesn't make too much of a big deal about it.

"You're quite full of shit for a little guy, aren't you?"

"I bet you haven't done some of the things I've done," I say and feel nothing.

He takes out a joint from his pocket.

"Malawi," he says.

We smoke it together, passing it between us after a few drags.

I start to feel high. The sky seems close, like I can touch the stars.

"So what's it like living under a bridge?" he says.

"You see the stars at night. If you stand close to the fence."

"So what, you live with homeless people?"

"We have a home. It's just not your normal kind of home with a kitchen and all that stuff but it's still a home."

We finish the joint.

"We better get some sleep," he says in a grown-up voice.

I hate it when they do that. It just changes everything. It's like they become something else. Sorry, I'm a grown-up now. Time to sleep. Fuck off, you cunt.

I go down first. I found the place, I say. I walk quickly in the dark and soon find my way into the tunnel. I can hear him behind me. He's big and tall and bumps himself. On the ground when he walks he isn't gentle. He makes the plants make a noise like a clumsy giant. In the cave it's dark. The fire is almost out. I see him at the door. He takes his big bag. "I'm going on top," he says. I don't say anything. I put on my jacket and zip it up to the top and lie on the ground.

I feel irritable and can't sleep. I go back outside and pull out more grass. I get some needles and put them in the dying embers. I blow hard. Nothing happens. I take more small branches and make another triangle on the old fire. I put the needles in carefully and more grass and forget about my visitor. I blow hard and only think about the fire. I must feed it, I'm hungry. It starts to burn. I feed it gently. It burns slowly, it's tired. I only feed it a little arm and watch it. When that's gone, I'll sleep, I tell myself. He comes back again. "Are you starting up another fire?"

"Why not?" I say. He doesn't say anything, he leaves. I hear him crunching the plants outside. He bumps his head and yells out. The fire burns slowly.

He won't last, I think to myself. The mountain will eat him up. It'll make him mad. It'll make all his friends mad. He'll stop coming to work and will only want to spend all his time on the mountain. His friends will think he's mad and that moffie guy of his, he'll leave him.

I watch the smoke rise out the cave. It's driving him crazy. That's why he couldn't sleep. I didn't ask him to come here. There's plenty of room on the mountain. Why did he have to come here? White people are full of kak. I watch the fire and ache to throw in a monster but it burns slowly so I leave it alone. I hope he goes in the morning, I think to myself. I can find that pool by myself. Just because they smoke with you, they think they can do and say anything to you. Well fuck you, asshole. Jou poes, man. Jou ma lek hol. The fire burns. I hug my knees and stop thinking about him. Who does he think he is?

The fire sputters and the cave goes a little darker. I must

137

sleep now, I say. Tomorrow I will swim. I'm going to destroy that water. I'm going to swim like it's my last day to swim, I say as I curl up to sleep. The ground is soft. I don't mind the dirt in my hair. The fire is my blanket. I close my eyes and drift.

17

In my dreams I walk all over Cape Town. I meet everyone I
know and they all say nothing to me. Their lips are sewn together with wire and they bleed. I see everyone I know except
Gerald. I even see myself walking up the mountain. My skin is
thin and looks like a lizard's with all the markings. I watch
myself crawling up the mountain. Along the way I meet a
crash of rhinoceroses. They ram over people and injure them.
My trail up the mountain is covered in blood. I follow the
blood path as I climb.

At the cave I meet a woman who looks like she lived a very
long time ago. She is short and her bum is big but she has the
lightest smile I've ever seen. She wears only a leather thong
and her long breasts are like fruit, like fat pears. She is shy and
hides in the cave. I follow her in, careful as I walk. She sits in
the corner of the cave while a small fire burns. I go inside and
sit next to her. I can't stop looking at her face. She has a beautiful face and a yellow skin that seems to glow. In the cave she
looks at home. It is neat. There are carved bones, herbs that
make you want to smoke them, clay animals and lots of other
small beautiful things. And the floor is the earth. It is the softest sand I have ever sat on. I play with it while I stare into her
eyes. They are big and sad.

"What's your name?" I ask her.

She begins to sob.

"Saartjie," she says and stops crying.

I throw some sand onto the fire. It sputters. She giggles.

"I have come from very far."

"How far?" she asks.

"Maybe over the ocean, I don't know."

"That is a very hard thing, not to know where you come from."

"It has always been like that," I tell her. "Do you live here alone?"

She starts to sob again.

"Forget that. Do you like swimming?" I ask her.

"I was once a fish," she says and stops crying.

"I was once a seal. I used to love water but then I got lost and now I'm here. Do you know the way home?"

"This is home for me. I don't know anything else."

I think about her answer.

"Do you know anyone else?"

She rubs her eyes and two drops fall from one eye.

"Forget that. You mustn't cry," I tell her.

"Will you be staying here long?" she asks and wipes her tears.

"I don't know but I like it here. I live down below."

"The city. I don't like all their noise."

"I know. I have been lost there for a long time. I'm trying to find my way home. They said I must find T-rex first. Have you seen T-rex?"

"Oh, you want T-rex?" she says and claps her hands with excitement. "He is out today."

"When will he be back?"

"When he's finished eating. He gets very hungry, T-rex, and there is nothing big here so he goes down below to eat the people."

"Does he eat children?"

"Yes, he eats everything," she says proudly like a mother, "he doesn't waste."

"Do you think he'll eat me?" I say, a little scared.

"No. But he will if you don't stay."

"Then I'll stay," I say.

"You know there used to be many T-rexes."

"How many?"

"Four."

"But that's not many."

"Have you seen T-rex before?"

"No," I tell her.

We hear loud thumping noises outside and the earth shakes a little.

"That's T-rex," she smiles coyly, "do you want to meet him?"

"Why?"

"He's my husband," she says, a little insulted.

I go outside with her and we stand on the roof of the cave.

Down below in the city we see T-rex stomping over cars and tearing apart buildings; chewing people but they can't scream because their lips are sewn together with wire.

"That's my husband," she says and squints to get a better look at him.

I watch him destroying the city and feel scared. We go back inside.

"So he's the last T-rex, then."

"No, you are, he's getting old."

"Me? But I'm still growing."

"I know," she says and looks at my scales, "you are going to be big just like him."

"Really?" I say and my eyes grow big.

"That is your father."

"Why didn't you tell me before? I've been searching for him."

"Because you never asked me," she scolds me, "you asked me where your home was."

"So this is my home?"

"I don't know. Do you like it?"

I don't answer her for a while.

"I like it here but I don't know where to sleep."

"You must sleep where you like."

"Can I sleep in here?"

"Of course, don't you remember? You used to sleep here."

"But where will you sleep?"

"With T-rex," she says and hides a naughty laugh.

"But I'm hungry."

She cooks meat over the fire. She adds herbs and other things that smell nice. I eat all I can.

"I was very hungry," I thank her.

"What else do you like to eat?"

"Sometimes when I'm really hungry I eat rats but they are not tasty."

"Why?"

"Because they just smell of piss all the time, even their meat."

She sighs. I can see she is a little sad but I keep talking to make her think about other things.

"I'm really tired," she says, "I must get back home."

I look at her sadly as she leaves. When I go outside she is gone and it is misty. So misty that you can't see your hand when you put out your arm in front. She must be quick, I think and go back inside. After a while Gerald comes in. He finds me cooking some meat over the fire. He sits next to me and tries to speak but his lips are also sewn together.

"Don't try and speak, your lips are bleeding," I tell him.

He makes muffled sounds and points wildly with his fingers.

"What, you're hungry?"

He nods.

"No, you can't eat."

He bleeds as he tries to speak. The blood drips to his bare chest.

"Oh wait. I can hear T-rex outside," I say excitedly.

The earth rumbles.

"I think he's calling you," I say and turn over the meat. It burns on a stick. Gerald goes outside. I follow him out of the tunnel. The mist has cleared. In the distance we see T-rex. He stomps and takes big steps.

"I think he wants you," I tell him and pat him on the back.

He shakes his head.

"You have to go. You know that, don't you? I'm too little to eat you. But I'm growing up fast."

He shakes his head.

I smack him with my tail and he falls. He cracks his head on a rock but still gets up. T-rex gets to him and chews off his head. Snakes pour out of his neck. He slashes them with his sharp nails and eats Gerald. I go back inside to finish cooking my meat. I put it over the fire for a while. When it's red and bleeding, I eat it.

18

I wake up feeling thirsty. It is hot again and the sun is up. I go outside and take off my jacket and pants. I put them on the slab of rock to air them and climb on the roof. The other idiot's left but I see he tried to make a fire. It's a small thing. I stand with my rough feet in the ashes and piss. The sun shines. I feel its heat on my face. Today I'm going to swim, I tell myself. I get down excitedly and wash at the stream. I think of nothing but swimming. I drink lots of water. Afterwards I put on my clothes and walk to the other side.

I pass tall grass and climb up rocks. My hands are also beginning to look rough. My skin peels but it doesn't bleed. From the highest point on the mountain I look around and go towards the hills. White people are everywhere. They think they own this mountain, I say to myself as I look at them eating Simba chips and drinking Coke. They point at things like they fear nothing. Look at this, look at that, I hear them say. Let's go here, let's go there. And they walk like they own the road. They don't look at the ground. They only look ahead of them. That's why animals are always running away from them when they try and see them up close. White people don't know fear and animals know that.

I walk on my own, the sun always behind me. I go down a steep path with railings and begin to see water, blocked by a long wall. I walk towards it. I get onto a bridge and walk. I get to the other side of the bridge and see the water. This is what that idiot was talking about, I think. I look around and there is no one. I take off my clothes and lay them on white rocks. The whitest rocks I have ever seen. The water is a dark brown colour. Near the water's edge tadpoles swim.

As much as I want to dive in I decide against it because there are rocks. They are beautiful but they are still rocks. I take a few strokes and swim out. The water is warm on top but below my feet feel cold. It must be deep, I think to myself. I don't swim far out because I saw water pouring out of the other side of the bridge. If I'm not careful the pump will suck me out. I cut into the water with my arms. I feel strong. I think of nothing but the water. When I float and look around, the water seems black. You can't even see your hands underneath. It's a bit scary but it's still water, I encourage myself. A man walks down the bridge towards me. I swim quickly back and forth, splashing everywhere.

"Excuse me," a coloured man says standing on the rocks, "you're not allowed to be in there. This is a reservoir."

I swim towards him. I get out of the water naked and go for my pants.

"Sorry, you're not allowed to be here. Regulations," he says as I put on my pants.

"Are you like the police here?" I ask as I look at the things on his shoulders.

"Something like that."

Why do grown-ups always say that? I'm not stupid. Why can't he just tell me what he really does?

"But it's hot."

"I know, but it's not allowed."

* * *

I stay on the mountain for four days. Every night I make a big fire in the cave. I burn all sorts of things, mostly arms and legs and lots of monsters. And every day I wake up early and swim at the reservoir before that man comes to work. I have great swims and learn to play with water alone.

At night I have strange dreams. I always see Saartjie. I remember one dream very well. I was walking near the reservoir at night with her. The moon was hiding. We made a small fire to see in the dark.

"Mantis is angry," she says to me with her big eyes.

"Who's Mantis?"

"He stays on the moon but sometimes he walks the earth."

"He must be able to fly."

"He can do anything. He made T-rex."

"Did he make you?"

"Of course," she says like I asked a stupid question, "he's my father."

147

"So why is he angry?"

We sit under a tall tree that looks like it doesn't belong there. She starts sobbing. I just sit there. After a while she stops crying and wipes her tears.

"I don't want to cry but things are difficult."

"What things?"

She shows me an old wound under her breast. I can see maggots crawling in the wound.

"Mantis," she says looking at the wound, "is very angry."

"I don't understand."

"The eagles stole my babies," she starts to cry again.

"Eagles?"

"They fed them to T-rex. But he didn't know they were his babies. That's why Mantis is angry," she says and sucks green at the back of her throat before continuing. "Mantis is very angry. Nothing can be done to change that."

Then, in my dream, I take out a small bone from her ribs. I use it to take out the maggots under her breast. Then I sew up her wound with some string. I tie another piece of string to the bone and hang it under the tree. We sit and watch maggots crowding round the bone. They become so many that we have to move from under the tree. We sit near the rocks and watch the reflection of the sky in the still water.

"Mantis is coming," she says, terrified.

When we don't expect it an old man suddenly appears.

"This is my father," she says sadly.

He walks with a long cane and his back is bent. His skin is dry and he has many wrinkles like someone was drawing lines on his face. And his eyes are like dirty water. They are murky and hold scary secrets. I watch him closely as he takes small steps.

"You must go back into the earth, Saartjie," he shouts when he reaches us. She starts crying.

I get up to greet him but he smacks his cane on the ground. My bum itches, so I sit down. I look at him with fear.

"You tried to cheat me," he yells with an old voice.

"It was his idea," Saartjie says and wipes her tears.

"And who are you?"

"My mother was a fish," I tell him in my dream.

"I ate her," he says carelessly. "Now tell me who you are!"

"I'm not sure," I tell him, "but they call me Blue."

"Sometimes when you're sleeping I swim in your eyes. It keeps me young."

"So you want to cheat death?" I challenge him.

He stares at me with the scariest eyes I have ever seen.

"I want to see T-rex. What have you done with him?" Saartjie suddenly demands.

"Nothing."

"Then why didn't he come back home tonight?" she starts crying again.

"She is always crying," I tell him.

"I drink her tears," he says.

"Why?"

He doesn't answer me and then says something strange.

"The stars have told me that you're the nothing. You eat anything and everything. You're always hungry and you're always thirsty. But you won't eat me. I am going to kill you."

"No! Go and leave Saartjie alone. The stars have told me. I can also hear them."

"You are the devil's child. Only a stupid man like that would have a child like you."

He turns around and walks back. He disappears into the night.

"Why are you still crying?" I ask her.

"Because you killed my father."

"But I was saving you. He was going to kill you."

"I didn't ask to be saved. You're not the only one who knows things."

We watch the fire. It burns slowly. Bats fly around us and disappear. A fish splashes in the water.

"I used to stay by the river once," I tell her.

"Why don't you go back?"

"It was a long time ago. I don't really remember where it was."

"What made you leave?'

"People. It's always people. They cut me up into little pieces and spread me everywhere."

We stay out for a long time but the sun never seems to rise in this dream.

"Mantis was so angry he stole the sun when he died," she says.

"Where did he take it?"

"He ate it. And it burned him to ashes."

Again we sit in silence.

"I will tell you a secret," Saartjie suddenly says. "You are the sun's child," she says and smiles.

"But Mantis stole it."

She looks at me and starts to cry.

"I'm tired," she says.

"I must go now," I respond and get up.

"You can't leave me alone," she tells me.

"What do you do when I'm not here?"

"I wait for T-rex," she smiles.

"Then wait for him."

"But I can't wait for him alone."

"Then who do you wait with?"

She looks the other way. I sit down angrily and dust rises.

I look at the water and feel angry for letting myself be here with her. I wait for her to fall asleep to make my escape but she never sleeps. She keeps talking to stay awake. She talks about silly things. I get bored and get up to take a piss. When I pee my water is bright yellow and starts shining and becoming fire. I pee for such a long time that my bright yellow water becomes the sun. When I get back it is morning and she is nowhere to be seen. I go outside to look for T-rex but he is also nowhere to be seen. So I sit on the roof and stare at the sky.

The sun warms up my scales.

19

After four days on the mountain I leave. I take nothing from the mountain except my jacket. It is cloudy, the morning I leave. And a strange icy wind that I've never felt picks up. I put on my jacket and walk for a long time before I meet some-one. The first person I meet on my way down is a Rasta. His dreads are long and fall over his shoulders. He walks with a stick which seems to have a life of its own. I look into his eyes and know that he is going to plot evil on the mountain. He looks back to me as I start my descent. You are evil, I say to myself and go down.

The next person I meet is a white boy with orange hair. He smiles and I see that his teeth are dirty. They are brown. He wears a white T-shirt with a blurry image of a runner. I try not to look at his dirty smile as he walks by. He has bad breath and smells of sweat. I go down further, the sun hiding behind clouds. I walk faster to warm myself up. I take off the jacket and turn it inside out. I wear the orange colour outside to attract the sun.

I meet other strange people who give me angry eyes when they look at me. They look at me as though they know what I have been doing on the mountain. Even though I look thinner,

I feel stronger and protected by an invisible silence. Something seems to walk with me as I pass them. A guy nearly trips because he looks at me with such hatred. I don't feel scared. I don't hesitate. I don't trip. I look all around me. I look above me and the sky is still quiet, holding secrets.

Eventually I get to the road which is at the foot of the mountain. I see a white car parked in the distance. I walk towards it. It looks like a white Grenada, Gerald's car. I go towards it and feel nothing. The windows have been tinted black. I get closer and all of a sudden the engine starts. The car revs before it drives off. It leaves a cloud of dust as it speeds down the road. I fear nothing, I tell myself, not even the dark.

I go down another path where the dead trees are. My feet guide me. I listen to everything. A thought comes to me: the dead trees are dead dreams. I wonder what that means? I think and keep walking. I scratch in my pocket and take out my money. Thirteen cents. I must have lost one cent on the mountain. I put it back in my pocket and keep walking. It is a nice walk even though the sky is sulking with clouds. I start to feel warm and open my jacket. The further I go down the warmer it gets. And it is humid too. When I get to the black rock I turn back and look at the sleeping mountain. A blanket of mist covers the top and moves to the edge. I see dragons and monsters when I look at its edge.

It starts to drizzle. I don't mind because I haven't washed.

The tiny drops of water feel cool on my face and chest. I close my jacket again. I walk past the little lake but no one is swimming. There are no families sitting around the tables. Water falls quietly. I can hear trees sighing with relief. They are thirsty. They have been thirsty for a while. The grass becomes softer and doesn't crackle when you walk on it. It just makes a soft shushing sound. I walk out of the trees till I get on the cricket field. The grass is green and short. There are no school children. I walk around the field and start to hear the city. Taxis hoot, dogs bark and in the distance the big boats burp like whales. I walk down a steep slide of dried grass. I climb down into a ditch that continues for a while. I come across a dead cat – there are flies and maggots all over its mouth and eyes. I step over it and get back onto the road. It is still drizzling. My jacket is my raincoat. I wear it with pride and my feet are warm.

I go towards the bus station to look for fruit that the hawkers may have thrown away. I look in a few discarded boxes and find a mango. It is over-ripe but at least it is still clean. I flick off three ants and start peeling it. My hands get messy. I think of the cave as I lick them clean. I think of that girl in my dreams. I can't forget her face. I eat the whole mango and clean the big pip, which looks like a head of blonde hair. I hold it in my hand and go towards the train station. I pass many people inside, all rushing to work. With so many people you'd think someone would bump into me. But no one does. They walk as though they know where they are going. I go to the Men's toilet. A row of men stand pissing against the wall. I go to a tap and wash my hands. Water drips. I go out and walk towards town. I pass Subway and go towards that busy road where town ends. I go between cars when the robots are red and go towards the bridge. I think of nothing but the sun. It stops drizzling.

I go to Liesel's first but her shack has been destroyed. I walk around and see quite a few other shacks have been destroyed. In the corner I can still see Gerald's shack but his car is not there. I go to Ma Zakes' spaza and find it closed. A woman with a baby strapped to her back walks up to me. She has terrible scars, railway lines running all over her face like someone wanted to change it. I look at her heavy eyelids. "Who are you looking for?" she asks.

"Gerald," I say.

She walks away. I go to the bench near the spaza and sit. I wait for a while before Sealy comes.

"What happened here? Half the shacks are gone."

"New blood," he says and sits next to me.

"Where's Gerald?"

"Didn't you hear?"

"Hear what?"

"He killed himself. That's what they say. They found a knife with blood in his room."

"What do you think happened?"

"I found this in his room," he says and takes out a claw from his chest pocket.

"What's this?"

"My oupa says it's a lion's claw."

"Did he scream?" I ask.

"Nothing, not a sound. He locked his room like he usually does when he goes to bed and then he never woke up. I had to break in there. It was a mess, what he did to himself. I still say no man would have cut himself up the way he was. You don't seem surprised."

"It's Gerald. He was going to die anyway."

"Apparently the Twenty-Eights had a contract on his head. But something else got him first."

"The darkness," I hear myself say.

"Look at all the people still here. Most of the coloureds left. You won't find a coloured guy here. Gerald was their god and when he died they all left. People have been spreading rumours all over Cape Town that the devil got him."

"What do you think?"

"I think he destroyed himself. He wanted to kill you, you know that? He was going to steal your soul to make himself stronger."

"I know," I say, "I burned him."

"Gerald was looking all over for you. He was going crazy. He started talking to himself. I like your jacket." He smiles and touches the orange material.

157

"So only darkies live here now?"

"Not exactly. After Gerald died I fucked up Liesel."

"Why?"

"She was a bitch. Did you know she used to put stuff in your zol?"

"Like what?"

"There was a lot of shit happening that you didn't know about. The day I fucked you up, Gerald wanted me to break one of your bones, so I made as if I broke your ankle and he fell for it. Shit, you even believed it. There was nothing broken about your ankle."

"But the doctors . . ."

"Fuck the doctors. Gerald wanted me to break one of your bones so he could sow his evil. But I fooled him to save you. I know you killed him," he says.

"What?"

"I know you went up to the mountain."

"How do you know?"

"I saw you. I flew up there," he laughs, "but I was the only one who could see you. The others weren't strong enough to fly up there."

"Gerald was evil."

"Gerald is the devil."

"What do you mean?"

"He's not dead. But he's weaker. You destroyed his power. Now he can't touch you."

"But how do you know this?"

"Because I'm an angel."

"An angel?"

"Yes."

"But . . ."

"The devil is not the only one who knows evil. I saved you by fucking you up. You're stronger now, aren't you?" he says.

"Yes," I say confused.

Ma Zakes opens her spaza and puts on some music. She plays that fuck-you song by Tupac. Gerald never wanted her to play that song. We were never allowed to listen to it.

"So what are you saying, that angels are evil?"

"No, I'm saying we can fight till the end. We can outlast the devil."

"But you said he's not dead."

"I know, but that doesn't mean he can win."

"Will he ever die?"

"I don't know."

"Are you bullshitting me?"

"Did I bullshit you when I fucked you up?"

"No," I say and remember.

I get up and go to Ma Zakes. I ask for a glass of water. She gives me a jug with ice blocks. I sit with Sealy on the bench and drink.

"Can he still hear you when you talk and all that other stuff?"

"No. He died as Gerald but he'll come back as something else."

"How many of you are out there?"

"Many," he says and takes out a cigarette. He gives me one. We smoke in silence and listen to Tupac swearing everything under the sun. Ma Zakes pumps up the sound.

"It's our turn to rule," he says after a while. He looks at me and swims in my eyes.

"You're mad," I tell him.

"Tupac was an angel," he says. "But he didn't know it because he didn't know his father."

"What?"

"Tupac was the angel of destruction." He bops his head to the music.

Two white men who look dirty walk past.

"When did they come?"

"Not long ago."

"They look evil."

"They are evil but they are harmless. They're like mosquitoes. They can smell your blood. But they can't do anything without spilling your blood and they can't do that."

"Why?"

"Because you burned yourself with fire."

"But I have no scars."

"You stopped bleeding, didn't you?"

"What do you mean?"

He moves his bum.

"How do you know?" I say, surprised.

He goes to Ma Zakes and buys a Coke. He comes back and sits next to me.

"God is very clever," he says seriously with a grown-up face.

"You believe in God?"

"I'm way past that. I know him," he says and drinks.

"You're full of shit."

"We have to destroy Cape Town," he says.

"Why?"

"God's instructions."

"But why Cape Town?"

"You ask that after what they did to you?"

I say nothing.

"It's because evil is subtle," he says. "Evil hides itself. Gerald was only scratching the surface."

"You mean he wasn't evil?"

"He was but there's worse."

"Where?"

"In the church, in banks, in town. That's why we have to destroy Cape Town. We have to rape their women and children. We have to kill them."

"You're crazy – that's evil."

"That's how you fight evil. With evil."

"You're mad."

"We're the dogs of war."

"Who's we?"

I see the other roughnecks as TKZee raps. The music makes you want to dance. Sealy gets up and dances with his buddies. I watch them and feel their mad energy. "TKZee is in the house y'all," they sing with the music. When the song ends they all sit around me.

"You must stay here now. We'll look after you," Sealy says.

"I can look after myself," I say.

"They'll take your strength."

"Who?"

"The Twenty-Eights, the Hard Livings. All the mother-fuckers and their mafia will try and take your strength. You mustn't be on your own," he says and holds my hand gently. "You must stay here now, you have no choice. They're all looking at you."

"Who's they?"

"Christians, Muslims, Buddhists, gangsters, the mafia, the government... who else do you want me to name? All of them are looking at you."

"What do they want?"

"They want answers."

"But I don't know anything. I'm only thirteen."

"They want to look into your head. They want to see what God's thinking."

"That's evil."

"But it still doesn't stop them."

"What can I do?" I say, exhausted.

"Nothing. But you must stay here."

"What if I don't?"

"What did Vincent say to you?"

I look at him and say nothing.

"He said, Ask questions that are going somewhere."

"How did you know that?'

"Because Vincent is an angel," he says without flinching.

"You're full of shit. You're filling my head with kak. How do I know that you're not another Gerald?"

"Am I holding a knife to your throat?"

"No," I say and look above. "Where are all the pigeons?"

"Gerald ate them."

My heart starts beating fast.

"You want me to lose my mind, but I won't," I shout.

"Shut up. You're making noise," he tells me. "I'll moer you if you continue like this. Now shut up, this is serious."

He foams at the mouth. The others watch me. They'll beat you up, I tell myself. I sit quietly in confusion.

"Are you hungry?" Sealy asks.

"No."

"Have you eaten?"

"No."

"Ag, voetsek," he says and gets up to dance.

"Are you scared?" one of the two asks. I look at them with cold eyes and squint at them.

"Sealy is right. You are crazy. You want death, don't you?" The other laughs.

"No, I think you're crazy," I tell them.

"We raped all their women after Gerald died. All the coloured bitches," he says to the others and they laugh.

"Why?"

"They wanted destruction."

"They wanted to meet their maker through the back door," the one with one eye says.

"You're all sick."

"We're mad with love," Sealy says, dancing and swims in my eyes again.

"I'm tired," I tell him.

He takes me to his room. He lights a candle and closes the door but he doesn't lock it. Gerald would have locked it, I say to myself and don't know whether to feel relieved or anxious.

I sleep with my feet on the bed. I don't trust them. Grownups are full of words. But they never tell you everything. They just tell you little bits of things. And that amounts to nothing. What are they talking about? All of a sudden they are talking about God. God this. God that. They are full of shit, grownups. Their minds are rotten with all their poisons. I know Sealy also smokes buttons. He is mad. He says he is doing it in the name of love. What must I do with that? Must I believe him? He is crazy. They're all crazy. They think they are God. They think they know it all – the score.

20

I watch the candle burn and think about the mountain and the cave. I wonder who's staying there now. Maybe that stupid man with long hair will come back. And he'll say, Where's that boy who's full of shit? But I'm not a boy. I know I'm thirteen but I'm not a boy. On the street boys my age support their families. They give their mothers money so that they can buy drugs and feed them nothing. They break into cars and steal small change from dashboards so that they can buy needles to inject themselves with poison. They mug old ladies and buy buttons. And when they are fucked out of their faces they cry about it till snot drips like water.

A boy? I'm not a boy. I've seen a woman being raped by policemen at night near the station. I've seen a white man let a boy Bafana's age get into his car. I've seen a couple drive over a street child and they still kept going. I've seen a woman give birth in Sea Point at the beach and throw it in the sea. A boy? Fuck off. They must leave me alone. I have seen enough rubbish to fill the sea. I have been fucked by enough bastards and they've come on me with enough come to fill the swimming pool in Sea Point.

And the bitches are all the same. You can't trust them. Where's

Liesel now? Wasn't she my friend? Didn't she say she liked me? She's also full of shit. And that story about her putting stuff in my zol, I believe it. I knew what a hard bitch she was but I just ignored it. I thought she was my friend. I thought she liked me. I knew how she made the woman called Kim who stayed with her suffer. When Kim was sick and couldn't work the streets Liesel didn't help her. She didn't give her any food. She let her starve because she was a hard bitch. I saw Kim scratching in the bin. And now everyone wants to fuck me.

But I don't want anything. I just want to be left alone. I just want to be able to walk the streets the way I like. I don't want to think about gangsters who are so scared that they fear their own shadow. I don't want to think about bastards who pick me up at night when their wives are not watching and fuck me for peanuts till I bleed. I don't want to think about bastards who do it in the dark with children because their dick is so small. I don't want to think about assholes who don't wash their ballas but want you to suck them till they come. I don't want to walk around being frightened all the time. I don't want to hear Gerald saying you have learned to live with fear.

What does that mean? It means grown-ups are evil and they use you and they use their children to use you. They use anything they can use and when they get it they still want more. They are never satisfied. I don't really remember a grown-up ever saying enough. They always want more. Even if that means you have to work till you die. Grown-ups are full of shit. They are evil. Why are they watching me? What do I have that they can't get from their own efforts? There's plenty of other things to steal. Why do they want to steal my mind? Why can't they do things for themselves? Why must I do all the work and some-one else must steal it? Grown-ups are devils. They have chil-dren so that they can feel good about themselves. So that they can say, I made you. I can take you out of this life, like my father once said. I never forget that. How can anyone say that? Grown-ups have children so that they can say, Oh God I'm going to come. I'm going to shoot all over you.

And why must they always have the first and the last word? Why must I always be in the middle? I didn't ask for trouble. Why do they want to fill my head with ugly things? I see ugly things all the time. Isn't it enough? Do they want me to see and think ugly things all the time? Must I become a stupid pigeon so that they can feel good about themselves? They are stupid. They are fucked up. They are crazy.

I try to sleep but sleep doesn't come easily. Instead I think of people watching me. I think of Gerald being torn apart by a lion. I think of him dying in his sleep. I think of blood, his blood and all the people he ate. I think of it spraying from his veins like a wild hosepipe. I think of his T-shirt burning him, becoming alive with fire. I think of all the stupid things he said and how he craved my eyes. They were the last things he couldn't have. He wanted my eyes, I say to myself and watch the candle. He wanted to be clean like my eyes but he couldn't. His own darkness killed him like the old man in the dream.

A long silence falls on me as I think about these things. And I don't have a good feeling about Sealy. He is full of madness. You can see it in his eyes. They are on fire, that's why he was swimming in my eyes. He's on fire with madness. And I can't go back to Sea Point because the grown-ups over there are even more crazy. I sigh and decide to stay under the bridge. At least they will feed you, I say to myself. Although nothing is ever certain with Sealy. He is like the wind. He changes his mind all the time. And those buttons, I don't want to see them anywhere near me. They are evil.

When the candle burns out I cover my head with a blanket and sleep. Later in the night Sealy crawls next to me. He smells of brandy. He wakes up at night to throw up outside and then he comes back smelling of buttons. I don't say anything. I just pretend to sleep.

* * *

I wake up feeling bad like I caught Sealy's hangover. His eyes are red and he drinks lots of water. We go in Gerald's car to Salt River. I sit next to him in the front seat. The place in the dashboard where you put in things is open. I can see a gun in there. It looks like a 9mm.

"What do you need that gun for?" I ask.

"Because you never know, Blue."

"Never know what?"

"You ask too many questions. That's why you're always in trouble."

I keep quiet.

"Maybe they'll try and kill you," he says.

"Maybe they'll kill you," I tell him.

"Look, I'm only trying to protect you."

We go into the coloured area and stop outside a house so rundown you can smell grease from the walls. I stand outside in the sun while Sealy goes in. He comes back holding a pack and tells me not to ask questions. Stupid questions, he says. We drive on a long road till we get to Muizenberg. We park at the beach. He gives the pack to other coloureds and comes back with a stacked envelope. We get in the car again and drive back into town. He buys me fish and chips with Coke. We eat in the car, parked near Subway.

"I'm just going for a walk," I tell him.

"Don't be stupid, only white people say that. Now where are you going?"

"To the park."

"To do what?"

"I just want to lie in the sun. What's your problem?"

"Then I'm coming with you," he says.

We go to the Gardens. I walk in front. I walk past the fountain where there are always lots of people. I can't help looking around and watching people. But they don't seem to be staring at me or, if they are, then they are doing a good job of pretending to do other things. We walk till we reach the tall trees. I lie under the sun and Sealy sits next to me. I feel like napping but I can't because he's always there. And I know he's watching me. So I just lie there and look at clouds. After a while he gets irritable and says, Let's go. I'm too tired to argue so I just follow him. We walk back to the car and drive to the bridge.

"So what's going to happen to Gerald's room?" I ask.

"You and your questions. Nothing, okay. Nothing," he says and gets out the car. He goes to his shack.

But what about the blood, I wonder. The rats will lick it, I suppose.

"I'm tired," I tell him.

"Then go to sleep," he says.

I go to his shack and lie on his bed. I don't think much. I just sleep. And I dream of many things. Easy things that make me sleep for a long time. I dream about the swimming pool in Sea Point and eating lots of ice cream.

I never dream of doing it with a woman. I'm not a moffie. One of the bastards once asked me if I was a moffie. And I told him that I'm not a moffie. But it's strange that I never dream of doing it with a woman, not even beautiful Toni Braxton. And the other guys are always saying that it happens to them. I just lie about it and say that it happens to me too even though it never has. But this doesn't worry me too much. It worries me that I have never done it with a woman and that I've only been doing it with men even though I don't like them. They're hairy and ugly. What's there to like?

When I was growing up I used to play with Vincent and the neighbourhood girls. We used to like playing house. Vincent used to like playing that game because he was always the father. And the father gets to do it with the girl who plays the mother. We used to play in the back near the dirty stream where there were no shacks. Vincent would go behind a tree with the girl. "We're going to sleep now, children," he would say and they would lie behind a tree in the long grass and do it. The others would do their own thing. Like I was always the brother and I would look after the others who were supposed to be younger.

Vincent always liked playing the father but the girls never liked playing mother when it meant that they had to go to bed with Vincent. They would soon come back and complain that Vincent's thing was too big. "But if you open your legs wide, it will go in," he always answered. Then we would all laugh and we would start another game where everyone shows each other their thing. I never liked this game because my thing was small. So when we played this game I would think hard of doing it with a woman till my thing was hard. The others would laugh and the girls would want to touch it but I wouldn't let them. But they never said they wanted to touch Vincent's thing because he had hair around it. He was the only one with hair around it. We all used to look at this hair with wonder and his big thing.

But one day Ma Ntando saw us and she chased us with her broom. We ran away, and since Mshenguville was big, she never knew where we stayed so she couldn't tell on us. Those were fun days. When Vincent was feeling naughty we would dodge school together after break and buy a cigarette at the shop. It was Vincent who taught me how to smoke and breathe out of my nose. But I would feel bad about missing school because every day I came home my mother would ask me what I learned at school that day. And I didn't like lying to her. She always knew when I lied and would give me a hiding. But about school I could lie till my teeth were green and she would never suspect.

So I didn't dodge school much with Vincent. I only did it maybe twice a week. And sometimes he would ask me to dodge with him on the days when the teacher was going to ask us to say the times tables. I used to hate dodging because I liked saying the times tables but I dodged for Vincent because he was nice to me. He would beat up the boys who beat me up because I had blue eyes. He was always my friend, Vincent. That's why

I used to dodge school with him. And in the neighbourhood everyone knew he was a rough fighter. He once hit this boy so hard that he bled through his nose. And you know what Vincent did? He licked the other boy's blood from his knuckles. After that everyone was scared of him, even some of the bigger boys. All the other kids wanted to be his friend but he chose me as his special friend. I never forget that. Sometimes when I feel down, I think of the day Vincent beat up the biggest boy in school because he was bullying me.

We were at the playground at break. Rotten Sibu saw me eating a lollipop and wanted it. I refused. He slapped me hard and grabbed it from my mouth. I didn't cry. I never cried, not even when my father beat me. Vincent came along like a dog with rabies and tackled Rotten Sibu. Like the giant he was, he fell. Then Vincent sat on his stomach and started laying in the punches. He punched him till the principal dragged him away to his office. He got ten of the worst lashings on his bum. I think he even bled. For weeks after that he couldn't sit on a chair without putting damp newspaper on his bum. He was my special friend forever after that.

21

I follow Sealy around wherever he goes. I have become his second shadow. Under the bridge there are mostly black people living now. A few of the coloured bitches stayed. But all the coloured guys left. And of course there are those two white men. They don't say much and only speak to the older people under the bridge. I never see them sitting outside Ma Zakes' just to have a drink or to talk. But I have stopped worrying about them. I used to think they were up to something. I'm not sure what I thought they were up to but I was suspicious of them. They seem harmless, like Sealy said.

And the police come in more often since Gerald died. They're always raiding us for drugs. Sealy has never been busted but he knows they are watching him. They are waiting for him to fuck up. They don't seem to mind the dagga that much. I guess because we don't sell that much. I mean, I've never seen anyone being arrested for a measly stop. But you can never be too sure with these assholes. They are capable of anything. I'm always careful when I smoke zol outside. I keep an eye out.

Sometimes when Sealy feels friendly he packs the car with his roughneck friends and we go to Muizenberg. We park outside the beach and set up a braai. With Tupac belting out of the car we eat, drink and dance. But I don't drink that much. When everyone is shit-faced and drunk I sneak out and take a walk with the seagulls.

There are always chip packets floating at sea. And I've heard that some of the skollies throw their needles into the sea or they leave them lying on the sand. You never find that sort of thing happening in Sea Point. There's always someone watching. And white people are full of shit anyway. If they saw you leaving your rubbish lying around they would probably tell you off or something like that. It's a pity because the water is warmer at Muizenberg.

I like watching people swim. There's a certain order about it. Out at sea there'll be one or two white faces, mostly surfers. They don't fear the sea. As always they go at it like they own the sea. And then still out at sea but closer to the beach you'll find the coloureds, laughing and frolicking in the water. I must say, no matter what anyone says, coloured people know how to have a good time. They just seem to know how to have fun. Wherever there's laughter and mischief on a beach, there's usually a coloured face not far from there. And then at the water's edge you find black people. We always seem to be scared of water. Usually women will be wading in the water wearing their swimming caps to protect the chemicals in their hair from reacting with sea water. And they like to wear tights and funny-looking swimming things. We dress funny at sea, black people.

You can always tell by how we dress that we are scared of water. Once I saw a woman with one of those air things around her arms and waist and she didn't even go into the water. She just stayed near the water's edge. But black men are a little more adventurous. They go in with the coloureds and have their fun. And black people always take home with them a bottle of sea water with sand. They drink it and do all sorts of rituals against evil with it. White people and coloured people aren't interested in that. Sometimes I see them collecting shells. And they like bringing their dogs to the beach even though you're not allowed.

Sealy says that a long time ago before there was land there was only water. And that everything, even people, lived under the sea. He said black people were the first to leave the sea and live on land and then others followed. And because we left the sea a long time ago, far longer than the others, we forgot how to swim and started to fear water. It made sense to me when I heard this. But it still didn't explain my blue eyes and my love of water.

* * *

Sealy goes to Salt River a lot. And he starts leaving me behind when he goes. I slowly watch him change. First he gets a gold filling in his front teeth and then he starts buying flashy clothes. And the kind with expensive labels. Arrogance grows in his eyes. When he looks at people it is with a sort of hatred. He even stops eating with me. He starts reminding me of Allen but doesn't have Allen's dirty mouth. I don't know who's worse. On the streets they start to know about him. I worry, as the police are watching him. He also takes a lot of other drugs, not just buttons. He sniffs cocaine and even smokes crack.

One night three police vans come in. They come straight to Sealy's room and wake us up in the middle of the night. In his room they find three parcels of cocaine and some crack. They beat him up badly and it doesn't help that he puts up a fight. Dogs also sniff around in other shacks and his roughneck friends also get caught. They take them away in their van and they leave the bridge screaming like demons from the back of the van. I don't sleep much after that.

The next morning four lorries come in. They wake up everyone and tell us that we are moving. They start taking apart shacks. The women scream and shout and swear. It takes about two hours for them to pack our belongings into the lorries. A bulldozer follows behind.

I give away all Sealy's stuff and vow to go back to the streets. They can go wherever they're going without me, I say to myself and leave as the bulldozer takes apart everything in sight.

I go to Sea Point. It seems like a long walk. I count to a hundred many times before I get there. I go to the moffie place at the sea and stand near the water's edge. The sky is angry with dark clouds. It rumbles and lightning flashes between clouds. I feel tired and lost. I stand there and wish the water would take me back to the sea but it doesn't. Huge waves come crashing down and white froth gathers at my feet. I look for the seagulls but they are nowhere to be seen. I stand there alone. My feet get wet. When it starts to rain I move. A painful arrow crawls up my legs and stops in my stomach. I haven't eaten. I feel weak but walk as the rain gathers strength. I have no place to go to, I say to myself and look at the mountain. It is also cloudy up there, dark moody clouds that look like dragons.

I walk towards Green Point, the rain on my back, but I have no energy to hide or to run. I just keep walking. After a while the rain falls at a steady pace. I pass Green Point and head into town and then I go for the hills. It rains harder. The wind starts blowing in my face. I struggle to go up. I reach the trees and continue walking. Raindrops fly into my face and get squashed. They are like little bombs. I walk further up and feel depressed. My mother has died. My father has died, I say to myself. I say it over and over like a song, a chant. The trees are wet. When I move past them more rain falls on me. I get to the beginning of the mountain and look up. It looks dark and wet and there are no cars parked outside. I watch raindrops falling from a great height only to smash into smaller drops on my face. I start climbing. My stomach has no chance to moan. It works with the rest of my body to carry me up the steep mountain. I start shaking from the cold but I keep walking. The higher I climb the harder it rains. I trip on a rock in the ground and fall. I bump my head against another rock and get a cut on my head. I bleed and my body feels weak. I pick myself up and continue. My clothes feel heavier. They are soaked with rain. My mother is dead. My father is dead, I say to myself again.

I keep walking. My head feels light, a little dizzy. The wind blows and I nearly fall backwards but it blows in the other direction again and saves me. I get to the top of the mountain. It is misty and it rains. How will I find my cave? I wonder and start walking towards the other hills. The ground is muddy and there is water everywhere. I slip and slide and fall. I pick myself up and keep walking. Lightning flashes. I nearly fall down a steep drop because it is so misty. Eventually I begin to see that I will never find my cave and start to look for the nearest place I can find to rest. I walk down a familiar railing and stay on a cobbled footpath. Further down the mist clears. I go past the bridge and head down a hill. I begin to see large rocks. There must be a place where I can stay, I say and fight the wind. Barbed wire is around the rocks. I climb over it and cut one finger. I bleed and suck my blood. I don't like blood.

I crawl up the rocks and go down the other side where there are more rocks. My feet are useless in the rain. They slide on the rocks. I have to use my hands more to keep myself from going with the wind. Just before going down on the other side

I find a crevice between rocks. It is quite thin. I squeeze in my stomach and go between the crack. Inside it is dark. I take out my lighter from my pocket and flick it but it is wet and doesn't work. I whistle and the sound carries. I hear flapping wings and get scared. It is dark and sounds deep in there but I have nowhere else to go. I must go in, I tell myself and feel my way in the dark. You're getting closer, I tell myself. The rain still falls on my back through the hole. My feet touch the bottom and it is more rock. I get on all fours and crawl in. Above, a little light sneaks in through the crack. I see something flying into the hole.

I start to shiver out of control. I take off my pants and jacket and wring them. It is cold in here. I dry myself with my wet pants and hold my lighter. I blow into it to dry it while I shiver. I blow for a long time. The light coming through the hole even disappears. It becomes completely dark.

A million things go through my mind as I stand there naked in the dark, my clothes around me. It is difficult to breathe, as if breathing in the dark is like breathing in monsters. You're going to be fine, I keep saying to myself and pray that my lighter will work but the wheel just keeps turning and nothing happens. I hold my clothes carefully and venture a little further but not too far. I get onto a dry patch and sit on the cold rock shaking the lighter and praying for a miracle. Without warning a spark flies out of it. I catch a glimpse of a deep cave. Just in front of me I see another drop. I move back with fright. As another spark flashes the sound of a hundred wings or more fills the cave. I flick the lighter on again and see another spark. I keep flicking it till a flame stays.

I crawl on all fours and go in front of me. I reach the edge and look down. It is quite steep but I can see the floor. I must get down there, I say. I leave my clothes and find rocks that lead down. I climb down carefully, still shivering. My feet touch soil. Above me I can see a blanket of moving wings. Bats, I wince and tell myself not to look up again. I walk on the floor and look for wood. I trip on stones placed in a circle and shout out with shooting pain. There are ashes in the middle. Wood can't be too far, I say to myself and walk further. It is a big cave. Around a corner I find broken branches and some logs. One at a time I drag them back. I build a triangle with little branches. I do it carefully as there isn't dried grass to light up. You can't fuck up, I say to myself and keep checking the lighter's fluid. There is still plenty of fire in it.

I light the branches and blow gently. The fire catches at once. Shivering in the dark I feed it slowly. I don't think about anything except the warmth of the fire I will make. I even forget my hunger. The branches catch fire quickly and flames start to dance. I start to see more of the deep big cave. As the fire grows I feed it more wood. I look around and see that in another corner there are more branches. I go towards them and hear the rain raging outside. Near the branches water trickles down a rock and a wind blows through. There must be another opening up there, I say to myself and start dragging heavy logs. I bring as much firewood as I can get. The fire grows bigger and even falls out of the circle. I open it up by putting the stones further apart. I start to relax when I feel the heat on my body. When the fire burns steadily I climb back up to the top to get my clothes and bring them down. I drape my clothes on a log and put it near the fire.

For a long time I do nothing but just sit with my arms around my knees and watch the fire. It becomes my blanket. I think of the bridge and the shacks as just nothing but splinters of wood and rubbish. Rats are probably all that's left of that place.

When the fire is near my height I get up and start walking around. My shadow towers above everything. I walk around just to watch my shadow move. It creeps along the walls like a ghost. On one wall there are strange markings. Someone drew stick people and they carry spears and run towards a cow. But the cow is drawn really well. I can see its horns and its tail. I look at the strange drawings and a funny thought comes to me. I start walking around the fire. I walk in a circle, driven by a strange sensation to move.

There's nothing else to do, I say to myself. I start clapping my hands as I walk. The fire burns and smoke rises, escaping in the hole on top. I walk faster and faster and start clapping to a rhythm. I clap and start hopping. And the hopping becomes skipping. And then that becomes bounding and soon I'm dancing. I clap and fling my arms around wildly. I can hear the bats above me. On the floor not too far from me I see their shit. I dance around the fire and close my eyes. I see a vision of myself running like a wind though a forest. I run so fast that the forest becomes blurry. When I open my eyes, the fire asks me to feed it. I put in a heavy log and little bits of fire float and spiral in the air. I start to sweat as I get warmer. I feel every muscle in my body as I dance around the fire. The fire gets bigger and stands tall. With a little wind sneaking through the other hole it makes a sound. It is the sound of dreams burning. I feel feverish with energy and keep dancing.

When I close my eyes I see animals running at a furious speed. I see rhinos, wild cows with big horns, elephants and even lions. They seem to be running away from something. I even see a swarm of birds that make a dark cloud in the sky. The earth comes alive with the sound of these running animals. I dance around the fire and clap till I start to bleed through the nose. I hold my head up and keep dancing. The hairs on my back stand upright. Like a snake, that sensation crawls up my spine and erupts in my head. I start prancing about, huge leaps around the fire. My body feels light. I only hear the sound of bats and the rain and thunder. My heart beats wildly and for a moment I think it will beat out of my chest and pop out of mouth. I dance till I'm so exhausted that I collapse on the ground.

The soil is cold and cools down my body. I lie there for a long time and listen to my heartbeat settling down. When the madness has left I get up and wipe my nose with my pants. I stare into the fire and still see animals running in a wild stampede. Trees fly into the air and reach for the sun.

When I start to feel hungry I take ashes from the edge of the fire and draw shapes on my body. I draw a circle on my chest and give it arms and legs like it is a ball of fire that can move. I draw under my eyes and down my cheeks. A strange feeling fills me. I feel like I've done this before. When I look at the drawings on the wall I just know that whoever drew them used their fingers. They used branches and feathers and other soft things to touch. I look at them and think of that girl in my dream but I forget her name. I only remember her beautiful moon face.

* * *

I find it difficult to sleep in the cold. I must stay awake, I tell myself and feed the fire the whole night. Later in the night I get so drowsy and tired that sleep drugs me. I start seeing things. I see Gerald burning in the fire and rub my eyes but there is nothing there. I see monsters and lots of animals running towards me. I startle when I even hear the sound of hooves coming towards me.

22

Sunlight sneaks through the hole. The fire burns low. I leave it to die. I put on my clothes and they are slightly damp and smell of smoke. My feet smell like a sewer and remind me of all the unfriendly places I've walked in. I crawl out of the cave. I haven't slept much. Bleary-eyed, I go outside and squint in the sun.

It is a sunny day but it feels unusually windy like the sky is up to something. It is holding a secret. A worrying feeling comes over me. I decide to look for water. I drink from a pothole. The water tastes funny and I can see red salt around the edges of the pothole. I don't drink much. From where I stand I can see the sea. It goes out far and meets the sky, its lover. The water seems flat. You can't really tell that it's water. It just looks like a blue plastic thing that reflects the sun and moves gently like a conveyor belt. I stare at it for a long time. Nothing comes to mind. I listen to the wind and sit on a rock.

I look around me. There's no one around. I like these quiet moments by myself where there are no grown-ups. Small trees bend in the wind and the grass blows in all directions. The rocks stay the same. They never move. They are like giants with strange heads from another world. Maybe at night when no one is watching, the rocks move. Maybe they walk all over the mountain. Maybe inside the mountain there are people living there and they also come out at night when no one is watching. It is a nice thought because it makes me forget about my stomach. My mother is dead. My father is dead. That ugly thought comes to me again. I stay outside till the sun rises above me.

All of a sudden the wind stops. In the distance huge clouds move closer but they don't come on the mountaintop. It all happens very fast and looks strange, like a magic trick. Below at sea I start to see the water moving, waves gathering strength. It begins to look like a storm is coming but it doesn't rain. There are just heavy dark clouds and the wind tossing waves. But on top of the mountain it is calm. It is unsettling to watch the sea coming alive while the sun shines up here. Waves start rolling in from the distance. I follow their rolling motion all the way to the beach. They start moving in over the sand and swallowing the beach. It is too far to make out if there are people on the beach.

A huge wave rolls in. I stand up as it is the biggest wave I have ever seen. It gathers strength and moves quickly. I hold my breath and watch it tearing across the water. The sun shines in spots on the sea but on the mountaintop it is calm and sunny. The huge wave crashes into the beach and floods the street. Another wave comes rolling in the distance. It looks bigger than the one before and moves at a faster speed. Faster, faster,

I say to myself as I watch this trick. I dig my toes into the rock as the wave crashes onto the road and nearby flats. Cars get washed away. The waves continue like this for a long time, each time gathering more strength and each time destroying more of the beach. Then the sky gets angry and starts flashing lightning. Quivering bolts of purple fall into the water and upset it. But it still doesn't rain. The waves get wilder and bigger.

When I look into the distance I see a dark cloud moving. It covers the edges of the water. I squint my eyes and watch this cloud coming closer and closer. It is a long cloud that stretches across the sea. A terrible noise like deep thunder fills the sky. It is a sound which seems to upset the air itself. Behind me I can hear birds flying in a panic. I look behind and see a swarm of birds in the sky. All types of birds gather like a dark cloud. I even see seagulls. And then bats fly out of the cave. Small animals run wild on the rocks. I watch the ground becoming alive with frogs and insects. I jump as a snake slithers past me. At sea the terrible sound is like an explosion coming closer, spreading its destruction. A furious wind sweeps ahead forcefully. I sit down as the wind flies past me. It is so strong that I use a rock for cover. It blows everything in its path. Branches snap. Through the side of the rock I look and see the tallest wave the sea has ever made. It rises taller than any building I have ever seen. I look away and close my eyes.

My mother is dead. My father is dead, I say to myself and

hear a booming explosion below that shakes the mountain. I crawl down quickly as rocks start falling around me. Trees are crushed by huge boulders. Everything seems to crumble. On the ground there are small animals everywhere. They run around in circles of terror. The sky is angry with darkness and purple fire. My heart nearly stops beating when I begin to see water at the edge of the mountain. I stop in my tracks and look at the remains of a roof and other debris floating near the water's edge. The heads of dead white bodies float like kelp. I look away as the water creeps closer. I start running towards the highest point of the mountain. Underneath I crush little frogs and lizards. Birds cry in the sky. There is just a cloud of confusion on the mountain. I run till I start seeing other people. They run and howl with panic.

And then the sky opens up. I stop running as the water is safely behind me and watch dark clouds coming apart. I stand on a rock and chase away some lizards. Above me the sun shines like the ruler it is. It dominates the sky with light. A ball of fire comes from it. It splits into smaller balls as it comes tumbling down at a mad speed. I crawl under a fallen rock and see balls of fire falling around me like blazing razors. Even though plants are wet from yesterday's rains they still catch fire. Animals run for shelter. I hear boulders crushing everything, branches snapping like twigs. In the distance I hear the agonising screaming of people being burned. The sky rains with fire.

My mother is dead. My father is dead, I repeat again. The deafening sound of destruction fills the air. I put my fingers in my ears and close my eyes tight. The mountain shakes and the wind tears through everything. Insects scorch while the fire rains. Lizards crawl under the rock with me. They jump everywhere on me with fright. I try to ignore them and keep my eyes shut. Soon the whole mountain feels like an oven. I lie there and sweat with fear. When I open my eyes briefly I see hooves, claws and feet running in every direction. A hellish explosion comes from the sky. When the fireballs fall from the sky they make a frightening sound like a powerful machine tearing through something alive. Nothing seems to escape. The sun rules and it is harsh.

I know what fear is.

I breathe in deep and hold it for a while. When I let go, I open my eyes. I have seen the centre of darkness. I have seen the slave-driver of darkness and he is a mad bastard. I know his secrets. I know what he does when we sleep. My mother is dead. My father is dead.

K. Sello Duiker was born and raised in Soweto, South Africa, and went on to study journalism at Rhodes University before moving to Cape Town. His varied experiences while living there form the basis of *Thirteen Cents.* He also wrote two other novels, *The Quiet Violence of Dreams* (2001) and *The Hidden Star* (published posthumously in 2006). Duiker was widely considered one of South Africa's most promising young novelists before his untimely death in 2005 at the age of thirty.

Shaun Viljoen is a professor in the English Department at Stellenbosch University in South Africa, and the author of a forthcoming biography of the writer Richard Rive.

CPSIA information can be obtained
at www.ICGtesting.com
Printed in the USA
LVHW091705210120
644287LV00003B/392